To the Honourable Miss S...

and other stories

To the Honourable Miss S...
and other stories
by
Ret Marut
a/k/a
B. Traven

With an Introduction by Will Wyatt

Translated from the German by Peter Silcock

Lawrence Hill & Co.
Westport, Conn.

Cienfuegos Press
Sanday, Orkney

English language edition published in the U.S. by
Lawrence Hill & Co., Inc., Westport, Connecticut
and in the U.K. by Cienfuegos Press, Sanday, Orkney.

Library of Congress Cataloging in Publication Data

Traven, B.
    To the Honourable Miss S—and other stories
    I. Title
    PT3919.T7A6   1981   833′.912   81-7222
    ISBN 0-88208-130-6   AACR2
    ISBN 0-88208-131-4 (PBK)

British Library Cataloguing in Publication Data

Marut, Ret
    To the Honourable Miss S... and other stories
    I. Title
    833’ .912/F/   PS3539.R/
    ISBN 0-904564-45-2

Manufactured in the United States of America

1   2   3   4   5   6   7   8   9   10

Contents

Introduction

There should, perhaps, be no introduction to this collection of
short stories. The man who wrote them was adamant throughout
his life that the only important thing about a writer was what he
wrote, that the details of his life and background, indeed any
biographical material, were utterly irrelevant.

I would like to state very clearly: the biography of a creative
person is absolutely unimportant. If that person is not
recognizable in his works, then either he is worth nothing
or his works are worth nothing. The creative person should
therefore have no other biography than his works.

So, the author himself would choose that the stories should stand
alone, to be read and enjoyed in their own right. Many readers will
wish to approach the stories in this way, but I hope that they will
not be affronted, as I am confident that the works will not be harmed,
by a few words about this extraordinary author.

Until recently, a few words about the author were all that were
possible. He had deliberately wrapped himself in a cloak of mystery
and defied all attempts to tear that cloak away. He had lived in

several countries and followed a variety of occupations under many different names. In each of his guises he had obscured the truth about himself through his passion for secrecy. And the links between the different chapters of his life had been carefully and ruthlessly torn away. The stories in this collection were all written in Germany between 1915 and 1919. The author called himself Ret Marut, a strange name and an invented one. The origin of the name is uncertain. One guess is that it was made up as an anagram of 'traum', German for 'dream'. More likely is that it was taken from Hindu mythology, in which a 'marut' is a kind of God. Maruts ride in shining chariots of gold, carried by the winds, and they are themselves storm gods, striking down men with their lightning and splintering the trees in the forest. Thus, Marut was a suitable name for a writer who believed that his mission was to blast away false doctrines and to cleanse society of its wrongs. There is a testament that Marut's friends knew that his name was made up but they did not know who he really was or where he had come from.

The first trace of Ret Marut under that name is in Essen in 1907. He was a twenty-five year old actor at the theatre there. Over the following years he acted in a number of German towns as a member of various local theatre companies. He was apparently no great success as an actor, for nearly all the parts that he played were small ones. But he travelled around Germany from Essen to Berlin, as far east as Danzig, and back to Dusseldorf, playing his modest roles and taking an energetic part in branches of the actors' union. In 1915 he arrived in Munich, where he was to stay for the next four years.

He had already begun writing stories and articles, and in Munich he set up his own publishing company and began a magazine called *Der Ziegelbrenner* (The Brick-Burner or The Brick-Maker). The magazine was, in format, the size, shape and colour of a brick. The bricks were fired by Ret Marut to comment upon the corrupt society in which he lived and to begin the rebuilding of a new and better world. Marut was aided in the publication of the magazine by his girlfriend, Irene Mermet, but he appears to have written most of it himself. The first issue came out on September 1, 1917. The targets at which these bricks were hurled were the war, then into its fourth year, and the capitalist society, which had brought the war about. Marut had a particular hatred for the press, which he considered to be utterly corrupt and to have misled the German people: 'One has to beware of their editorials as of venereal disease.' *Der Ziegelbrenner's* subtitle was Criticism of Current Conditions and Disgusting Contemporaries, but this criticism was only occasional, for the magazine appeared at irregular intervals.

Marut, as revealed in *Der Ziegelbrenner*, was hectoring, romantic, capricious, full of exaggerations, obsessive, a man shot through with a desperate idealism. He was shouting angrily at society from a seat on the sidelines.

I cannot belong to any party because to be a member of any party would be a restriction of my personal freedom, because the obligation to follow a party programme would take away from me all possibility of developing into what I consider to be the highest and noblest goal on earth: *to be a human being.* I do not want to be anything but a human being, just a man.

This overriding belief that the single individual human being was paramount did not prevent Marut from remaining an anonymous figure himself. He would give no personal information to readers of *Der Ziegelbrenner* and in reply to one reader he wrote, "I shall always and at all times prefer to be pissed on by dogs, and it will appear to me to be a greater honour, than to be pissed on by readers of *Der Ziegelbrenner* with letters that attempt to sniff out holes in my garment in order to pin me down, for no one else has the opportunity of boring himself into my flesh."

For Marut, the message was everything: 'I have not the slightest literary ambition. I am not a writer, I shout. I want to be nothing but—the word.' On one occasion he organized a meeting under the auspices of the magazine, and when it came to his address, the lights had to be turned out so that he could not be seen.

Most of the stories in this volume date back from this period of Marut's life. They were all published under the name of Marut, with the exception of 'The the Honourable Miss S....' which came out under the *Der Ziegelbrenner* imprint, but with the author's name as Richard Maurhut.

By the end of 1918 *Der Ziegelbrenner* was sounding a euphoric note. The issue of November 9, 1918, was entitled 'The Day is Dawning', and the issue of January 30, 1919, was headed 'The World Revolution Begins'. Munich was in turmoil. As the war dragged on, its unpopularity increased, particularly in Bavaria, where the Independent Socialists, implacable in their opposition to the war, began to flourish at the expense of the Majority Socialists. On November 7, 1918, a huge rally in Munich was addressed by a number of socialist speakers, one of whom, Kurt Eisner, urged the crowd, which included many soldiers, to occupy the military barracks and seize weapons and ammunition. The result took everyone by surprise. The following day, King Ludvig III fled, and Eisner was in charge of a government which had declared Bavaria a republic. Eisner's idealistic, but eccentric and chaotic government lasted only a short time. In January he suffered a crushing defeat in elections for the Bavarian parliament and although he held on for a few more weeks, he had no choice but to throw in the sponge. He was assassinated on his way to tender his resignation to parliament.

Eisner's death was followed by a period of havoc during which three factions competed for power. The Majority Socialists, who were forced out of Munich to set up a Bavarian government in exile in Bamberg; a Communist group; and a band of anarchist intellectuals by Gustav Landauer, Erich Mühsam, the poet and playwright, and another poet, Ernst Toller. When this group formed a Republic of Councils (*Räterepublik*) on April 6, 1919, Ret Marut joined them and took a seat on the committee set up to produce a revolutionary propaganda and censor the press. Not that Marut's uncharacteristic move into prominence and action lasted very long; the Republic of Councils itself existed for only six days. But when soldiers from Berlin attacked Munich on May 1, 1919, in order to destroy the revolutionary government there, Ret Marut was one of those captured. According to an account which he published in a later edition of *Der Ziegelbrenner*, he was picked up and put with a group of prisoners who were being summarily tried and shot. Through the good agency of a sympathetic soldier he managed to escape shortly before his turn in front of the judge and succeeded in leaving Munich and going on the run.

Marut was accompanied on his flight by Irene Mermet. They

were at various times in Vienna, Berlin, and finally Cologne, where they stayed with a group of artists, the Kalltallgemeinschaft, among whose members was Franz Wilhelm Seiwert. Seiwert completed several portrait drawings of Marut and illustrated the last issue of *Der Ziegelbrenner*, which was published from Cologne on December 21, 1921. Marut and Mermet crossed the German border into Holland and probably travelled together across the Atlantic to Canada, where Marut was refused entry. He recrossed the Atlantic and landed in England in August, 1923. At the end of that year he was arrested in London—he was an alien and had failed to register with the police. He served time in Brixton prison until he was released in February, 1924. He left London some time in April that year. One way or another he arrived in Tampico, Mexico, that summer. On his departure from Europe he abandoned the name of Ret Marut, never to use it again.

When he arrived in Mexico, he began calling himself T. Torsvan and also Traven Torsvan. He took odd jobs in the Tampico area and began sending back stories to Germany under the name of B. Traven. The first stories to be published there were 'The Cotton Pickers', which appeared in the leftist newspaper *Vorwärts* early in 1925. A book club of the left, the Büchergilde Gutenberg, liked the stories and got in touch with Traven through a post office box number in Mexico. Over the next eleven years the Büchergilde published *The Cotton Pickers* and nine other novels by Traven, as well as one nonfiction book about Mexico.

Two other novels followed from other publishers in later years, and throughout this time his books were translated into many languages, but there was never any certainty as to exactly who B. Traven was, for he would give none of his publishers any details about himself or his background. There were no publicity photographs available to inquirers, nor any biographical material.

He seems to have lived under the name of Torsvan in Mexico, at least until the early 1940s, when he began using the name Hal Croves. It was under this name that he introduced himself to the Hollywood film director John Huston, who was making a film of Traven's book *The Treasure of the Sierra Madre*. Croves was present throughout the filming, acting as technical adviser, but he passed himself off as Traven's friend and agent, although there were some who guessed that he might be the author himself. He continued under the name of Croves until his death in Mexico City in 1969. Throughout this time he denied that he was the writer B. Traven. When some readers spotted a similarity between the spirited, antiauthoritarian books of B. Traven and revolutionary journalism of *Der Ziegelbrenner*, he denied also that he was Ret Marut.

It is clear now that Ret Marut, T. Torsvan, B. Traven and Hal Croves were one and the same person. Traven's books chronicled the struggles of the poor and the dispossessed of the world, often with an allegorical and legendary quality. *The Death Ship* is the story of an American sailor who finds himself abandoned in Antwerp without papers to establish his identity. No one believes that he is who he says he is, nor even that he is an American as he claims. He travels through several European countries before finally hopping on board a broken down freighter, the *Yorrike*, a ship doomed to be sunk by its owners in order to realise the insurance money. He teams up with a Polish colleague, Stanislav, and they escape from the *Yorrike* only to board another ship, which suffers the same fate as that planned for their first boat. There is a jaunty and devil-may-care feel to much of the story, as well as a dark and vivid glimpse of the harsh life below decks on an ancient cargo boat. The book is a hymn of praise to those who work in such places and to their unquenchable spirit.

Traven's most famous book, *The Treasure of the Sierra Madre*, is an allegorical tale of men's lust for gold. It is both a stirring adventure tale and a satire on greed. A later series of books, often called 'The Jungle Books', tell the story of a peasant uprising in Mexico, in which the poor workers of the mahogany forests challenge the harsh dictatorship of the time. It is clear on which side Traven's sympathies lie in this conflict, but he never quite throws his hand in behind anyone's solutions for the troubles of the world. He is simply on the side of the individual who searches for a decent way of living in a harsh and unjust world.

Recent discoveries have shown that Marut/Traven was not an American, as he always claimed, nor a Norwegian, nor a Swede, nor any of the other nationalities ascribed to him, but that he was, in fact, a German, born on February 23, 1882 in what was then the far eastern corner of Germany and what is now Poland. The town of his birth was Schwiebus, now called Swiebodzin. What we have learned of his early life throws an interesting light upon some of the themes of his writing. His father was a potter, and at one time worked, interestingly enough, in a brickworks, possibly the source of Ret Marut's inspiration for the name of his magazine, *Der Ziegelbrenner*.

His parents were unmarried when he was born, and the young Marut/Traven, whose real name was Otto Feige, was brought up for the first few years of his life by his grandparents. He seems to have retained a feeling that his grandparents were, in fact, his true parents and later developed this into the idea that he could choose who his parents were, that he could choose what his real identity was, that he could decide to be whoever he wanted to be. This doesn't explain in any simple way his political notions or his psychological obsessions, but it does fit with Marut/Traven's strong belief in the individual's power and right to do and be what he wants, and with his own refusal to give details of his birth and background, either when he was living as Ret Marut, or, later, when he was the admired author B. Traven. The young Otto Feige seems to have been a lonely, withdrawn child who kept to himself and felt apart from his family and those around him. He was deeply upset when he was taken from his grandparents and returned to his real parents. He was disappointed again when his parents prevented him from studying to become a priest, because they could not afford to support him while he did so. In his early twenties, soon after his national service in the German army, Otto left home and cut himself off from his family, never to see them again. In doing so, he reinvented himself as the actor, and later writer, Ret Marut, creating an identity of his own choosing, abandoning the accidents of birth and parentage. His family knew nothing of his later careers and travels, save for two letters that he wrote from London when he was in trouble with the police there. Even then Otto kept his new identity hidden from them, and they learned nothing of what he was doing or what he was calling himself.

The stories in this collection are all from the Ret Marut period of the man's life. 'Deceivers' is particularly interesting, in that it tells of a mother who protects her son so much that he is kept from games with his friends, kept from the profession he wishes to follow and kept from taking the political action that he thinks right. All three of these constrictions seem to chime with the life of Otto Feige. He had few friends as a child, he was prevented from studying for the priesthood and he did row with his family about his socialist politics. His sister Margarethe, who died in 1981, told me that the young Otto had practised political speeches to himself in the family home and had collected pamphlets and placards with which he intended to hold political meetings in their small village in Lower Saxony. His mother had been angered and alarmed by her son's socialism, and it was soon after a row about this that Otto left home never to return. 'Deceivers' can be seen, perhaps, as a justification for a son's breaking away from his family and his background. The man in the story is trapped by his mother's possessiveness. In 'Mother Beleke', too, the power of a mother's influence looms large. Otto Feige's mother was from all accounts a powerful and domineering woman.

Several stories touch on a theme which clearly affected Marut strongly and which were certainly demonstrated by him in his Traven years. Many times in his correspondence with publishers, critics and readers he proclaimed that public taste was arbitrary and fickle and that the publishers' taste was no better. Although he was bashful to the point of obsessiveness about himself and his identity, he was in no way modest about the value of his work and was ambitious for its recognition and success. He blamed the professionals—publishers, critics and librarians—for being too blind to promote his work widely enough; and the public for not preferring his work to that of his inferiors.

In the story 'Originality' the actor only achieves fame, and more than that, an extraordinary triumph, when he does something really silly: performs the play in an utterly random order. Only then does he receive the unanimous acclaim of the critics, audience and fellow theatricals. Marut's scathing view of their taste may not be unconnected with his own failure as an actor, and, perhaps, with his own irritation at the success of other writers before he himself achieved what he considered his due recognition.

Certainly, in his Traven days he liked to view himself as a single, clear, true voice rising above the babble of his confused times. In the story 'A Writer of Serpentine Shrewdness', he takes a similarly low view of the public's literary taste. Fashion and pretention, he seems to be saying, are the arbiters of success for writers, rather than honesty and ability. Publishers have no worthwhile view of quality or even of commercial possibilities. In his early letters to the Büchergilde Gutenberg, Traven boasted often of the authenticity and honesty of his work and was highly sensitive to any suggestions that what he had written could be improved. He had a later altercation with his American publisher, Alfred Knopf, which concluded with his buying back the plates of his books.

'The Blue-Speckled Sparrow' was the title story of a collection of many of these tales when they were published under the auspices of *Der Ziegelbrenner* in Munich in 1919. It has the same chirpy tone of some of Traven's books from Mexico and in its theme—the humbling of a mighty decoration, which is made worthwhile, cleansed even, by being given some simple practical use in theatrical costumes—it mirrors the admiration for simple practical tasks which Traven displayed in his books about the Mexican Indians.

Marut's belief in the fragile nature of power, the ridiculousness of setting one man in authority over another—a common view in both *Der Ziegelbrenner* and the Mexican books—shines clearly in the story 'The Actor and the King'. In this, the simple suggestion that the King needs crowds of subjects to acknowledge him as King just as much as an actor needs to be surrounded by extras to imagine himself a king is enough to destroy the royal confidence. Marut, I think, often liked to see himself in the role of soothsayer. He relished the idea of bringing the whole house of cards tumbling to the ground with one simple and shattering insight.

When he arrived in Mexico and changed from Marut to Torsvan and took up the name of Traven for his writing, he became much influenced by the simplicity, charity and purity of the tales of the Mexican Indians. He used many Indian folk tales in his work, and 'The Silk Scarf' in this volume appears as a forerunner of that kind of storytelling. It's an extremely simple tale, but there is a splash of acid in the conclusion. Marut spits out the end of the story as if the sharp, bitter taste of injustice can be borne no longer. The cruel irony was to be used with even greater effect at the end of some of his books.

The stories here published for the first time in English provide an invaluable insight into the early work of a difficult, mysterious and suspicious man, but a man who never became used to the taste of injustice. Traven celebrated the brotherhood of all men and women and despaired, often with a sad smile, of the selfishness of rich and poor alike. In these stories he sings out with that clear and ringing voice which was often clumsy in expression but true in its note.

WILL WYATT
March 1981

To the Honourable Miss S...
and other stories

The Story of a Nun

The county town of Ley an der Nahe lies most comfortably situated in the midst of a landscape as fine as any that can be imagined. But as time goes by even the darkest of forests and greenest of meadows begin to grow tedious. Particularly on winter evenings. And when civilized men and such as presume themselves to share that distinc-tion have no better prospect in view, they sit down together and drink beer. One glass after the other. Between whiles, as is the custom of these parts, they drink an occasional mug of Rhenish wine. The advantage of such an alternation is that less time and effort are required to attain the intended purpose. But before the first messengers of the craved condition herald their appearance, the attempt must be made to while away the intervening period in whichever manner demands the least possible mental exertion. That, assuredly, is the most problematic aspect of the whole affair, and equally the most regrettable, because strictly speaking it is quite simply a profanation of the true purpose.

So it was that we sat foregathered: the postmaster, the veterinary (the doctor who administered to the human population was a married man), the apothecary (who was himself a married man, as it happened, but still he joined us because his children were already full-grown), the magistrate, the probationary teacher (who was constantly moving on, so that his replacement was amongst us before we had time to memorize his name), and a retired colonel who owned a country seat in Ley. Each evening a new topic came up for discussion. Which it did, except in the literal view of things.

The topic was certainly a different one each time, but on close inspection the subject matter proved to be the same as that which had already been discussed exhaustively the evening before, though in different terms and following a different order of precedence. One evening, however, the physician appeared in our circle. The new guest made his presence felt at once, in that the conversation turned to a new topic which had never been mentioned before.

What happened was that the magistrate greeted the doctor with the words, 'Well, now, Doctor, don't tell us you've been allowed the latchkey as well!'

For a moment it appeared that the doctor was about to fly into a rage, but he composed himself swiftly and said, 'My wife is away from home and I am afraid to remain in the house by myself.'

'So that's why you've come to join us?'

Here the colonel entered the conversation: 'Eh, what's that you say? You're afraid? Afraid of what?'

'Of ghosts,' the doctor said, with no trace of levity.

He did not allow himself to be disconcerted by the subsequent burst of laughter, but on the contrary repeated what he had said with the same grave solemnity.

'A doctor who believes in ghosts is something that even I have never come across before,' the magistrate managed between laughs.

'You would not laugh so readily if you knew the reason for my fear of ghosts. Believe me, I could heartily wish that I did not believe in them myself, but unfortunately it cannot be so. And because it shadows me at every turn, I never go out alone after nightfall. And that is also why you find me in your convivial company, to which it would hardly be proper for me to introduce my wife. Though of course you will be thinking that she keeps me on a short leash.'

'Indeed we do,' the apothecary confirmed.

'Then you are quite wrong to suppose that,' the doctor protested. 'It is entirely my fear of ghosts which prevents me from going out alone in the evenings.'

'Yet you must often be called out at night to visit a patient,' the postmaster remarked.

'That is quite a different matter. I have to draw the line somewhere. All the same, what I have to endure on such occasions is not something that I would wish on my own worst enemy.'

'Look here, Doctor, let's not beat about the bush, we all know that ghosts simply don't exist. As a physician, as a man of science, in a manner of speaking, you must be familiar with all the evidence against them.' By now the magistrate had also become rather more solemn.

'Certainly,' the doctor confirmed. 'Ghosts do not exist, as I well know, yet I have seen one with my own eyes. No, no, you need not pull such incredulous faces. I do not have trouble with my nerves, and at the time I was as completely sober as I am at this moment. I was still a student then, and as the holidays approached I began to look around for some small country town where I might find peace and quiet to study and go fishing and swimming, the sort of place that would offer the additional advantage of enabling me to live cheaply.

But because Gross-Zilchow was unaccustomed to catering for outsiders such as myself, who wished to avoid staying at a hotel, I found some difficulty in obtaining a room privately. The few furnished rooms available were most jealously guarded, and when a teacher or an official of the town council was transferred elsewhere, invariably his successor would already have requisitioned his room.

So it was that the proprietor of the hotel where I was spending the first couple of days drew my attention to the convent. The fabric of the building dated back to medieval times. It had been erected by an order of monks and had been occupied first by the reverend brothers and later by an order of nuns, until it came to serve the profane purposes of Lemberger the corn chandler. Herr Lemberger put the ground floor to use as a granary, while allowing the upper story to remain in its pristine and romantic condition, apart from a few of the old monks' cells which he had furnished and rented out to the employees of his firm, and others which were used as guest rooms whenever his sons invited their student friends home for the holidays.

For some time all went well. But one day a bookkeeper declared that he could no longer bear to live there, such was the fearful row made by the monks and nuns in the night hours. As if it had needed only this stimulus, all the youths who stayed there now came forward with similar complaints. Often, if the evening were well advanced, they would not dare to return home, much preferring to seek lodgings for the night with any of their acquaintances rather than enter the convent late in the evening. They also said that many of the young men who had left Herr Lemberger's service had done so only because they would then avoid having to live in the building, though not one of them had ever admitted the true reason, since they were afraid of being laughed to scorn.

Naturally I did not believe such humbug, for otherwise there would have been little cause for me to study medicine. The opportunity to stay in such a romantic building was not without its own peculiar charm, for the convent had been built in the early Gothic style and was a delight to look at. Its great halls, broad stairways, and spacious corridors were nothing if not tranquil. To work there would be a pleasure, true ecstasy in fact.

And so I went to see Herr Lemberger.

'I am more than willing to rent you a room, young man,' he said, 'and will let you have it for next to nothing. You may breakfast with us and need only give a generous tip to the girl who will tidy your room. I am sure you will find nothing to quarrel with in that. But as to how long you will last out there, well, that's quite a different story.'

'How d'you mean?'

'You see, the place is haunted at night by monks and nuns.'

'Who haunt it?'

'The old nuns, don't you know.'

'No, really? That must be a sight worth seeing. Herr Lemberger, I'll take the room. Most definitely. I'd like to meet one of these nuns of yours. It's not every day one gets the chance.'

'Just don't be too confident, my young friend.'

'But what do you take me for? I am a student of medicine, you know. Just you wait and see what a merry dance I'll lead those spirits and spooks. I'll soon scare them off for you.'

'If you can manage that, I'll lay on a first-rate champagne breakfast.'

'Agreed, Herr Lemberger, it's as good as done.'

'Very well, agreed. If you want to, you can move in later on today. I'll see to it that the room is made ready for you at once.'

That same evening I moved into the convent.

Although it had been my intention to return to my room by nine o'clock on that first evening, I stayed out until midnight. The fact that I was brave enough to want to live in the convent soon made itself known throughout the little town. The table in the Golden Ring where I sat that evening was besieged by a host of gentlemen wanting to make my acquaintance. The upshot was that eventually the most spine-chilling ghost stories were told, and made to seem all the more authentic by the circumstance that each had been experienced personally by a grandfather or grandmother of the narrator.

It was in a flesh-creeping frame of mind that I made my way home.

It would not have surprised me in the least had I encountered a monk or some similar figure on the stairs or in the spacious hall which occupied the ground floor. What did come as a surprise, rather, was that nothing whatsoever happened to me on that first evening, the one evening which would have been suited as no other to the explanation of some ghostly apparition.

I continued to live there for a full week without any untoward experience. Interest in the affair was substantially on the wane. The fame which I had initially acquired as a fearless hero was visibly declining amongst the local populace. That day—it was a Sunday—Herr Lemberger had invited me to dine with him and took the occasion to make the joyful announcement that he considered me the winner and would lay on the promised champagne breakfast on the following day.

That afternoon I walked for hours on end through fields and meadows. Then I returned to my room to put on a clean pair of boots before taking my supper in the garden of an inn.

I arrived home just as the clock in the church tower was striking eleven. Slowly and a little wearily I made my way upstairs. My thoughts were preoccupied with a fishing hole which had won the fulsome commendation of the gentleman with whom I had shared a table earlier in the evening, when suddenly I was gripped by the weird sensation that there was someone behind me on the stairs. I turned round but could distinguish nothing through the darkness. Standing motionless, I heard a muffled panting, as if someone were carrying a heavy burden up a steep path. And when I turned to ascend the few remaining stairs, I heard once more the laboured dragging footfall of the unseen visitor. On the topmost step I paused. Yet again the asthmatic wheezing filled my ears. Then all was silence.

I went to my room, lit the lamp, and shone it out into the corridor. Then with the lamp in my hand I went to the head of the stairs. Naturally I found nothing. Finally I persuaded myself that I had been tricked by my exhausted nerves into imagining some illusory presence.

Next day I requested that the champagne breakfast should be postponed. Taken aback, Herr Lemberger asked if anything was the matter. I excused myself by pretending a hangover, whereupon he said that we should not be cheated out of it, he did not dispute my victory, and an occasion would surely present itself to make hearty work of the champagne breakfast at some later date.

The following evening I entered the convent at ten o'clock. Though I could not bring myself to admit it, it was nonetheless true that my nerves were somewhat on edge, and that was why I was returning to my room rather earlier than I might otherwise have done.

Scarcely had I climbed to the third step of the stairway when once again I heard the shuffling gait of some unknown being behind me. With all the resolve I could muster I was attempting to convince myself that this eerie sound proceeded from the ancient worm-eaten stairway, when it took but a moment for me to dispel any doubt but that the stairs were not constructed of wood at all, but of red sandstone, and that their deeply worn surfaces bore witness to their venerable age. Instantly I cast about for some other explanation, but none came to mind. And though it seemed to me as if the stairway stretched into infinity, nevertheless I found myself instantly at the top without any clear memory of how I had managed to negotiate the final stairs. Once on the landing, I believed, of course, that the weird apparition would vanish without a trace, as on the previous evening. But this time the dragging footfall pursued me down the length of the corridor and was lost to hearing only when I opened my door.

As soon as I felt myself safely harboured in my room, it was only to be expected that I should try to imagine some natural circumstance to which the affair might be attributed. In the end I construed the footsteps to have been by necessity an echo, or at worst a reverberation, of my own footfall. But on the following evening this explanation was thrown to the winds. I heard the footsteps behind me on the stairs, then still behind me in the corridor, and holding to my explanation of the previous evening believed them to be merely the echo of my own. But once I had opened my door, just as I was turning to close it, I had the chilling sensation that someone was trying to force an entry to the room at the same time as myself. Quickly I pulled the door closed behind me and locked it from the inside. For a moment I stood listening and was on the point of lighting the lamp when the breath caught in my throat. Mine is not a timid nature, but had I been able to see myself in the mirror, I would have taken myself to be a ghost more dreadful than any that could possibly have been outside in the corridor. For quite distinctly I heard this mysterious creature pause for a moment on the far side of the door, then sigh deeply before finally returning to the far end of the corridor to descend the stairs with a weary and shambling gait.

That night, for the first time in my life, I slept behind a locked door.

In truth, I ought at that point to have moved out of the room. But I went on in fear of ridicule, all the more so since I was a medical man. So I remained where I was. My life and limb were in no danger, I supposed, never having heard that ghosts—though for the time being I still refused to believe in them—had ever inflicted physical injury on any living person. So it was my nerves alone that stood to suffer, and there I felt able to defend myself. Not that there is any difficulty in that, as long as one knows to expect something, however hideous it might turn out to be. The assault on the nerves that is dangerous is always the one which is sudden and unexpected, and I was expecting the very worst there could possibly be.

Again on the following evening the mysterious being followed me to the door. Slipping quickly into the room, I closed the door and once again heard the sigh. Yet at the very moment when I heard the creature move away, I threw open the door and shone an electric torch along the corridor. Nothing in sight. 'Is anyone there?' I called loudly. A deathly silence. I went to the head of the stairs and directed my torch down into the stairwell. Again there was nothing in sight. Again I called out. No reply. I returned to my room and stood listening behind the door for a moment, only to hear a woman's voice say plaintively, 'Yes, there is someone here.' Despite my understandable agitation, I wrenched the door open and shone my torch swiftly to left and right, though of course there was still nothing to be seen. Yet again I called out as before. No reply. As I closed the door, I heard the footsteps go slowly and wearily towards the stairs. So I had passed by whatever it was in the corridor without seeing it. For that is where it must have been standing, in the middle of the corridor.

I did not believe that an invisible being was capable of giving me an intelligible answer. Very well, I would assume that what I had supposed to be the reply of the unseen creature was no more than the echo of my own similar words resonating in my mind.

Naturally, the same thing happened again on the following evening. But perhaps I was rather more punctilious about closing the door than I had been on previous evenings. At all events, no sooner had I made it fast than I was overwhelmed by the feeling that whatever was there had just pressed past me into the room and was now standing alongside me within those very walls. Had I surrendered myself to the dread which threatened to possess me, I would surely have lost my reason. For long before I could have raced the length of the corridor and then down the stairs, not to mention the business of unlocking the main door, I would have succumbed. At such moments of horror it is always the best course to remain calm and to suppress as forcefully as one can the rising sense of panic. It is much easier than it might appear. The attempt itself is sufficient to provide enormous strength and to divert one's thoughts. When the horror returns to make itself felt for a second time, it is scarcely a fourth as dangerous.

I pulled myself together, reflecting that flight was pointless and would only aggravate my fear. The first thing to do was to procure a light.

The lamp lit, still I could see nothing. I shone the light into every corner, below the table, under the bed, inside the wardrobe. Nothing to be seen. Nonetheless, the sensation that I was not alone in the room was becoming more and more intense. To distract myself I opened a book and began to read. For some time I did indeed manage to divert my thoughts, but all of a sudden I sensed an almost imperceptible breath of air against my cheek. I turned around to see behind me a shimmering wraith of light that was endeavouring to assume human shape. Though the light from my lamp seemed to dwindle into darkness, as I leapt to my feet I was able to distinguish a woman dressed in a surplice, her fine auburn hair uncovered and falling over her shoulders in tresses of burnished gold. The thought that came to me in that first moment was that I really ought to have been overwhelmed by stark terror, to have cried out and taken to my heels, or have fainted with the horror of it all. But, strange to say, I felt not the slightest impulse of fear, which may well have been due not least to the circumstance that the nun had nothing of the apparition about her, in fact she appeared to be a warm-blooded and natural human figure whom one would simply have passed by, had one encountered her in the street, without suspecting that she merited attention in any way. Indeed, I felt confident enough to reach out my hand and touch her, thinking to satisfy myself that the woman was after all a living person who might have found her way into my room through some concealed doorway. But as I took a step towards her, she moved away in order to elude my touch. In that way I was able to go on believing that she might yet belong to the living and that I had no reason to be afraid of her. But, as I have mentioned, not the slightest hint of fear entered my mind. I would have felt entirely at my ease in conversing with her; I could even have invited her to afternoon tea without any sense of revulsion. What did hold my attention was the profound sadness in her eyes, which at the same time held the promise of a sensuality more ardent than any I had discovered in a woman before. Her face and her body bore no trace of ghostly emaciation; they were replete with the freshness of youth and concealed something which could not have failed to beguile me into the most abandoned ecstasy at some less haunted moment.

For a long time we looked at one another. I was able to study every single line of her features and impress them ineradicably into my mind. But at the very moment when I was about to speak to her, she dissolved into that shimmering wraith which had first made her visible to my eyes.

Once more my lamp was burning brightly, I was standing four-square in my room, and so could not possibly have been dreaming. I felt the sweat burst from my pores.

In spite of everything, I fell asleep the moment I got into bed, and slept soundly and peacefully until morning.

On returning home the following evening I heard no sound either on the stairs or in the corridor. I closed the door and lit the lamp, wondering what the coming night would hold in store for me. It was then that I heard a sound in the room, as if someone were undressing and getting into bed.

I turned around and on my bed there lay—the nun in her night-gown. Her head was pillowed on the auburn waves of her hair, her eyes were resting on me with passionate longing. I could clearly see the deep impress made by her body in my bed. She raised her arms and spread them wide, and in that instant the bed was empty. And the sheets were undisturbed as ever.

All the same, I had seen the pillows bulging as she lay on the bed.

At no time during the past few days had I let slip a word of what I had experienced to a living soul. I will readily admit that I was afraid to enter the convent once night had fallen, and more than once I asked myself whether it would not after all be better to move away from there. In the event, it was a lively interest in what might still lie in wait that proved increasingly persuasive. I had become frankly curious to see how it would end. And then I also entertained the slender hope that I might succeed in discovering some natural explanation for these occurrences, a task that would be all the easier the less I allowed myself to be swayed by fear. It is always fear which accords to the uncanny event a power that is difficult to overcome.

On the following evening it was again quite late before I returned to my room. It must have been shortly before twelve that I unlocked the front door. This was always a very slow business, since the ancient design of the lock made it cumbersome to turn. I had locked the door again and was turning to make directly for the stairs, when something compelled my glance to the right, drawing it further into the great hall through which I had to pass. The light of the moon was dazzling; milk-white rays tumbled into the hall through high lancet windows and suffused it with a pale greenish light. In the hall there were massive stone columns which supported the high Gothic arches of the vaulted ceiling. My glance happened to fall on one of these columns, and there, hanging from an iron ring embedded in it, was the nun, clothed in the same nightgown she had worn the evening before when she had lain in my bed. I recognized the nightgown at once, for it was embroidered with an old-fashioned design in faded yellow thread that contrasted markedly with the pallor of the woman's skin. On her feet she wore bright green slippers of medieval pattern. Her hair, its reddish hue seeming even more dazzling today than it had the day before, hung loose about the lowered head. Her eyes were closed. But what seemed curious was that the woman's face, so completely animate the night before, was now that of a corpse.

When I saw the woman hanging there on the column, my impulse was to run. But at the same time I remembered how awkward it was to turn the lock. Before I should have it open, I would have been devoured by fright. So I stood my ground. Naturally, my first thought was that the moonlight was refracted so remarkably in the windows that this image was being cast onto the column by rays of light. This led me to believe that I had discovered at a stroke an adequate explanation for the whole affair. I switched on my torch. Since its light was brighter than that of the moon, the sinister image ought now to have faded, had it in fact been caused by the play of refracted moonbeams. But the image did not fade; on the contrary, the stronger light of the torch made it appear all the more solid. As I edged a little closer, I was able to see that the woman's cheeks sparkled with tears recently shed, and also bore the traces of countless other tears.

On that night, too, the woman vanished as mysteriously as on the previous evening. I went over to the column and examined it scrupulously by the light of my torch, though of course I found nothing other than the embedded ring. For that matter, it was the only column to have been furnished with such a ring, the purpose of which I could not fathom.

I do not know where I found the courage, but nonetheless I went up to my room. Nothing whatsoever happened to me either on the stairs or in the corridor or in my room itself, although I had reckoned on it with certainty.

On the following day I discovered from a citizen of the town that there was in existence a chronicle of the convent, preserved in the municipal archives. While I was not permitted to take the chronicle home with me, I was nevertheless allowed to read through it in the council chamber. In it I came across a passage which implied in verbose and abstruse language that a young sister of the order, who had entered the convent against her will, had taken her life on the last night of a novitiate of two years' duration rather than endure a life in holy orders. She had hanged herself from the ring on the second pillar to the right of the main door. On the day after, the young son of a patrician family to whom she was said to have been bound in love had also ended his life by taking poison. The novice was described as having been very beautiful, though most beautiful of all was her abundance of auburn hair.

So far, gentlemen, mine has been a quite pedestrian ghost story. There is scarcely anything of note to be found in it.

I had still to experience the most sinister part of it. And actually it had nothing at all to do with ghosts, yet was more hideous by far than all that had gone before.

I had made the acquaintance of several people who had lived in the convent before me and questioned them about what they had experienced and seen there. Those I asked were also able to provide me with all the information that they had managed to glean from their predecessors, so that I was consequently able to collect a great many details. What was curious was the following. All those who had stayed there could relate only that they had heard footsteps dragging behind them and had the constant feeling of someone accompanying them up the stairs. Not one of them had ever seen anything.

In spite of that, I moved out of my room and booked myself back into the hotel. A few days later I went walking in the forest. Coming to a pleasant spot, I lay down and began to leaf through a book which I had brought with me. Yet I did not settle to my reading, but instead observed the tiny beetles as they scurried over the moss. Then I sensed that I was being watched intently. I looked up and saw—my nun. She was standing about ten paces from me, holding her hat in her hand, a girl in a thin, finely worked summer frock who was studying me closely.

My immediate thought, of course, was that here was my apparition from the convent again, still flickering through my memory. For there could be absolutely no doubt. I had the woman's features fixed too exactly in my recollection for there to be any possibility that I was deluding myself. Her face, moreover, was much too uncommon and singular. It was one of those faces which are glimpsed only once yet never forgotten, nor ever encountered again. And the glowing auburn hair, so strange and inimitable was its colour, could only have belonged to my nun. And to no other.

But suddenly, while I was still gazing at the woman in amazement, she lowered her eyes and blushed furiously. I could see that she wanted to run away, but something was holding her back. what that might be I could not tell.

Slowly she raised her eyes and said with a teasing note in her voice, 'Good morning!'

I was so taken aback to hear her speak that all thought of returning her greeting was driven from my mind. But then she came closer, held out her hand, and said once more, 'Good morning!' And when I still hesitated, she seized my hand raffishly, gave it a hearty shake, and said, 'Well, aren't you going to say good morning to me? Why not? We do know each other, after all.'

I felt the firm pressure of her warm hand and noticed that her embarrassed blushes were fading as her natural colour returned, yet I could see that she had the eyes of my nun, deep and melancholy, glowing with impassioned fire.

Surely the person before me was bursting with life, quite as fully alive as myself. So I returned her handshake and said, 'Good morning!'

'At last!' she replied. 'Though it took you the devil of a time, seeing that we know each other so well.'

'We know each other? Do you mind if I ask where we met?'

'Where indeed? Now that you ask me, I can't honestly say. I assumed that you would know. It's just that I feel we know one another, have done so for almost a fortnight. But then, if you say you don't know me, I suppose it must be right enough that I'm mistaken. Though truly I can't explain how I came to be mistaken. Perhaps it was just a dream that I had. All sorts of silly things can sometimes happen in dreams, can't they?'

Since I had taken a liking to her, I said, 'But there's nothing to prevent us from being good friends from now on, is there?'

'Gladly, for my part.' Such was her reply, given with cheerful candour.

She was the daughter of a family of prosperous clothmakers who had lived in that small town for centuries. Her father had died long since, her mother three years before. She lived with an elderly aunt and an aged servant in a charmingly situated house which she had inherited together with a sizable fortune. I visited her soon afterwards. My attention was caught by a life-sized portrait of her which hung in the drawing room, yet when I expressed my curiosity about the costume she was wearing in the picture, I learnt that this was not, in fact, a portrait of her, but that of an ancestress who must have died many hundreds of years before, for the picture was very old and looked so fresh only because it had been retouched a few years previously. Beside it hung the portrait of a man, apparently of the same date. What struck me about his face was the singularly marked angularity of the chin.

In the days that followed we often went out walking together, and almost every evening I was a guest in her home. Before I left the town, she consented to be my wife. She was beside herself with joy. I hurried to take my examinations, and one year later we were married. Our life together was full of happiness.

Her aunt died soon after we were married. We sold the house. I wanted us to keep possession of it, since we had no need of the money, but she pressed the case for selling with an eagerness that I found inexplicable, so persistent was she. She advanced every possible reason to justify the sale, until finally I agreed, for it was, after all, her own property.

Since then it has always been in my mind that had we not sold the house, we might have avoided all that was to follow. Maybe so. But then some other factor would have turned up to speed the course of destiny. That is something it is fairly safe to assume.

We had been married for a year and a half when my wife asked me if I would care to spend some part of my annual leave in visiting her birthplace. She wanted to see the haunts of her childhood once more and to place flowers on the graves of her parents. Perhaps her vanity was also involved, insofar as she wanted to show her erstwhile friends how happy she was.

We made the journey to the little town and took rooms in the hotel. But on the following morning my wife asked if we might move elsewhere, since staying at the hotel was not to her taste. Now both of us had cause to regret that her house no longer belonged to us. She would have liked to stay there again, but the house was occupied. Humorously I proposed, 'We could always move into the convent. Herr Lemberger would be only too pleased to accommodate us.'

It startled me to hear my wife say, 'It was the convent and only the convent I was thinking of when I got the feeling that I couldn't bear to spend another night here in the hotel. With all my heart I would dearly wish to stay in the convent. Even when I was a child, that was my one and most fervent desire. I feel that I would be at home there. Anyway, didn't you live there for a time before we were married?'

'Yes,' I acknowledged.

'I would so much like to see the places you knew before I met you. It always seems to me afterwards that there is more intimacy and trust between us when I see the surroundings you used to live in, where you have left something of your innermost self behind you.'

It made no difference that I told her the convent was haunted. She decided that she would not be frightened. The time was long past since she had been afraid to enter the convent, and then I would be there, too, and it would be so wonderfully peaceful there, with no one to disturb us, we could live there in just as much seclusion as on a desert island.

We moved into the convent. Herr Lemberger furnished two rooms for us: the one I had occupied previously and another situated adjacent to it.

Herr Lemberger accompanied us as far as the door. There I paused to exchange a few casual words with him. In the meantime my wife had already gone ahead. When I came to follow her I looked for her at every turn of the stairs, believing that she had concealed herself in fun since she did not know which rooms were ours. It was impossible that she should have guessed that the rooms in which we were to stay were the two at the far end of the corridor. So it came as the greatest surprise to me when I discovered her in my old room, where she greeted me with the words, 'This used to be your room!'

'How can you possibly know that?'

'I have the feeling that I have already been in here once before, but that must have been a very, very long time ago. There, just where the modern wardrobe is, there must be a niche in the wall where the prayer stool used to be in the past. Won't you please look and see!'

'You will be mistaken, my dear. I'm sure that wardrobe must have been in place for a great many more years than you can lay claim to.'

'Please, just for my sake, take a look. In the dome of the niche above you will also find a sturdy hook where the crucifix used to hang.'

'How long ago is "used to"? Surely you must know?'

'I really can't say, but it was a very long time ago.'

'Very well,' I said, 'I'll move the wardrobe out of the way and then you'll see that you are definitely mistaken.'

The wardrobe was empty and so could be pulled clear of the wall without difficulty. I found the niche, and the hook as well.

That same day I asked Herr Lemberger if my wife had perhaps been inside the convent during the time when she lived in the town. He thought it so unlikely as to be out of the question, but at the same time not entirely possible that his daughters, although much older than my wife, might have taken her there to let her see inside the convent. The furniture, and particularly the wardrobe, had been in place and undisturbed for thirty years, having been left to him by his father.

My wife was familiar with every cranny of the convent and could identify the purpose of every room, while I for my part did nothing to prevent her from spinning the most fanciful romances around every triviality. Not that I was able to ascertain what part of them was historically accurate and what was not.

We went out each evening without fail, either for a stroll or to visit acquaintances of my wife's.

We had spent about a fortnight there when I proposed that we should now move on elsewhere or at least move back into the hotel. Quite frankly, I no longer felt myself at ease in that eerie building, although I could hardly say that I had experienced anything out of the ordinary. I had forgotten the earlier occurrences entirely and was becoming more and more convinced that my nerves were overwrought as a result of the deathly hush within the building, aggravated by the thought that we were the only residents. But my wife would not hear of resuming our travels, any more than she would consider leaving the convent. She said she could not move away, for otherwise she would begin to pine for this building; first she would have to grow weary of the place; it was already beginning to bore her somewhat, and it would assuredly not be long before she had had enough of it to last her a lifetime, then her childhood longing would be stilled.

So we continued to stay there after all.

Several days later, as we were about to go out together, my wife suddenly urged me to go alone, saying that she wished to occupy herself with her reading. Although I returned home at an early hour, the daylight had already faded. Our room lay in darkness. I assumed that she had left it for a moment. The lamp lit, I turned around and on the bed there lay—the ghostly nun from my previous visit. I recognized her at once. Her body was clothed in that same nightgown with its singular old-fashioned embroidery of faded yellow thread. At the foot of the bed were the bright green slippers which I also remembered. My first thought was: Where can my wife have got to? But the nun stretched out her arms importunately and looked at me through eyes that were melancholy yet smouldered with passion. I saw the russet waves of her hair and the bulging pillows on the bed. I was turning to go to the door and call my wife when the nun said, 'My dear, come and give me a kiss, won't you? Are you annoyed with me because I went to bed so early?'

I turned pale, I knew it, and my heart skipped a beat—it was my wife. I went to sit beside her on the edge of the bed. My nerves were getting the better of me, I told myself, I would have to do something to calm them. But then I noticed the strange nightgown. My wife guessed the meaning of my questioning glance.

'You're wondering about my old-fashioned nightdress, aren't you? The embroidery is very old, you know. I sewed it onto the cambric myself, which is new, as you might guess. You do so like antique things that I thought I would do it to please you, and you won't find such wonderful embroidery as this anywhere in the world nowadays, that's for sure.'

'And the green slippers?'

'They were also handed down from my great-grandmother's day, or even earlier.'

'But you've never worn them until now?'

'No, and I haven't the faintest idea what it was that prompted me to bring these old things along with me. But them, you see, I came across these old clothes one day in one or another of the boxes that used to belong to my parents. In fact, it was mostly the clothes that put me in mind of the convent and how I would like to live here with you for a time. Just imagine, where we are now used to be inhabited only by nuns, and maybe a man has never kissed a woman here before. Isn't it terribly amusing to let your thoughts dwell on that kind of thing? I also believe that these old clothes have preserved a life of their own. I drifted off to sleep just a moment ago and what do you think? I dreamt that I was due to take my vows as a nun the next day, and the surplice was laid out and ready. But I didn't want to become a nun, because what I really wanted was to marry you and I was so terribly in love with you. Then I leapt out of bed in the middle of the night, because I heard you whistle a signal to me from outside the walls, and you were going to set me free and carry me off. But when I went down to the door, I found it locked and became quite desperate, and then all I could do was to stand by the pillar weeping bitterly, because I had to become a nun and you were outside signalling in vain.'

'And what happened then?'

'Then I held a little picture of you in my hand and pressed it to my lips again and again, and that was when I woke to find you in the room, and I was glad that it was all no more than a bad dream.'

I comforted her and soon we thought about it no longer.

Three days later, or it might well have been four, towards seven in the evening, I received an urgent telegram requiring me to interrupt my holiday at once and return home by the first train on the following day, since the next-to-senior physician at the hospital where I worked had contracted a serious toxaemia and no immediate replacement could be found for him. Immediately I set off for the station to buy the tickets and reserve seats, and also attend to several other small matters. In the meantime my wife was seeing to all the other arrangements and returned home before me to pack the suitcases. By the time I got back she had everything in order. For the last time we made our way down to the Lembergers', in order to spend the few remaining hours of the evening with the family. My wife soon felt tired, so we took our leave and returned to our rooms.

I had been smoking a good deal, and my head was in something of a whirl. So I said to my wife that I would walk in the street for a while longer, to catch a breath of fresh air.

The cool night air left me much revived. My spirits improved and I hummed and whistled to myself. Then I remembered my wife's dream. I thought to make a joke of it and went round to the rear of the convent, signalling my presence by whistling like an infatuated schoolboy. My wife appeared at the window, drew the curtain aside, nodded to me, reached her arm through the lattice, waved, and called down in a low voice 'I cannot come, the door is locked.' She was already in her nightgown and seemed to be on the point of retiring for the night. I was pleased that she had entered into the spirit of my joke so quickly and meant to speak a few teasing endearments to her once I had returned upstairs.

At length I entered the convent.

In the most cheerful of moods I opened the door. Meticulously I locked it behind me. Making for the stairs, I glanced into the hall. Involuntarily, my thoughts returned to that evening when I had discovered the nun hanging from the pillar. The moon was shining just as it had then, though perhaps not quite so brightly, since the sky was partly clouded over. And what I had almost been hoping for actually occurred. The nun was hanging from the ring embedded in the column. Just as she had before. The green slippers brushed against the floor. The yellowish embroidery of the nightdress stood out clearly against the pallor of her skin, her eyes were closed, her hands folded, and her auburn hair gleaming like cold fire.

I passed her quickly and ascended the stairs to our rooms. The lamp was burning and the curtains billowed in the draught as I entered, for the casement had been left ajar. I turned to the bed. By all appearances my wife had already lain in it and had then risen again. I shone a light out into the corridor and called her name. There was nothing to be seen and nothing to be heard. Taking the lamp with me I ran down the stairs and shone it around the entrance hall, only to see the nun hanging from the column. I passed by her as I ran to the small door at the rear of the building. It was locked. Then I raced back and, passing the column, brushed against a solid human cadaver—that of my wife! For hours on end I attempted to revive her. In vain. She must have been weeping only a short while before, for the traces of her tears furrowed her damp cheeks. But what cause had she to weep? The most nonsensical speculations were noised abroad. Even the state prosecutor took a hand in the affair. The rumour had emerged that a rejected lover from former days had first ravished and then strangled her. Others said that she had taken her own life out of homesickness, being loath to leave her birthplace for a second time.

The mysterious part of it was that her hands were clasped so tightly together that they could be pulled apart only with difficulty. When I finally managed to do so, in one of her hands I found a small porcelain miniature bearing my portrait. Whether because of some artistic caprice, or because the firing of it had been done ineptly, my chin as it appeared in the picture had acquired a singularly angular shape which I thought familiar. I pondered where I might have seen that remarkable chin before. And then it struck me: it was the same chin as that of the man whose ancient portrait had been hanging next to that of her ancestress in the drawing room of her parents' house.

Since that time I have been a prey to fear. That also accounts for the fact that I was married again only four months later, to my present wife. I could not have borne the solitary life for any longer than that. And now you will also understand why it is that I never attend your social gatherings of an evening. I do not want to leave my wife on her own, not for a moment longer than my profession will allow.

No doubt you would wish me to provide you with an explanation, where there is no possible explanation? Whatever interpretation is placed on the affair, it cannot be anything but speculative and so undeserving of the least reliance, unless one chooses to lose oneself in flights of baseless fancy.

And now, gentlemen, it is a quarter to midnight, and I must be away to the station. My wife is returning by the last train, and I wish to meet her. Thank you for allowing me to spend these past hours of the evening in your company, it would have been impossible for me to have remained at home. I bid you all good night.'

The Silk Scarf

The two of them, Karl Heppner and Klara Egeleit, were busy with the haymaking. Both were servants in the same village, to different farmers whose broad meadows lay next to each other. The summer sun blazed fiercely down on them, and when it was time for the two young people to unwrap their midday meals, they came together beneath the solitary tall and shady oak which grew on the boundary between the two meadows.

'Let me have a piece of bacon,' said Karl, 'and I'll give you a piece of my salt pork; it's a very fine piece.'

She cut a thick slice from the bacon and said as she gave it to him, 'Hold on, I'll give you a proper slice of bread to go with it, I know you men always have big appetites.'

'Your master doesn't exactly spoil you either,' he said, once he had examined the bacon and savoured its thin chicory sauce.

After that they had nothing more to say to one another. Leaning against the sturdy tree trunk, they sat chewing and gazed listlessly over the shimmering expanse of meadows and fields. When they had finished eating, he lit the stump of his cigar. She took the scarf from her head and tidied her hair. Then she spread the scarf over her lap and smoothed it out neatly. With seeming indifference he studied her as she did so. But while he was watching her in this way, seeing her arrange her hair and then stroke and fold the scarf with delicate gestures, inclining her head as if in scrutiny now to one side and now to the other, a strange sensation swept over him. It seemed to him that a gentle pulse of sunlight was pressing itself easefully into his bloodstream.

And in a voice rather more gentle than was usual for him he said, 'You know, Klara, I'm just this minute thinking how it would be if the two of us were to get married; wouldn't you say that we two ought to get along quite nicely with one another?'

She blushed and lowered her head further towards the scarf which lay across her knees, stroking it with increasing deliberation. A smile passed over her lips.

He sat where he was, entirely motionless except that he had turned his head towards her, and after a while he said, 'Hm! Well, what do you say to it, should we give it a try, the two of us?'

'Oh, yes, I'm very fond of you, too,' she answered, without looking up.

'Right, so that's settled then, Klara.'

She stretched out her hand to him and nodded. And then he said, 'I'll see that you're well provided for, Klara. I can do a good day's work, I'm not a drinking man and I don't throw my money about either, and when you and I come to set up house together, things should turn out well enough, don't you think?'

Then it was time for the two of them to go back to their work. That was all. No tears, no cries of delight, no kisses, and no sentimental speechifying.

On the following Sunday they went into town. 'Well now, I'll have to see about getting you a wedding present,' he said cheerfully. She laughed and said nothing in return. After a while they found themselves standing in front of a shop window in which was displayed a magnificent silk scarf of fine and vibrant colours. Irresistibly he was reminded of the way she had folded her plain headscarf so tidily and how this had made him feel that he would very much like to have the girl for his own.

'How about that silk scarf, would you like to have that?' he asked encouragingly.

'Oh, but heavens, heavens! It's much too dear for the likes of me and much too fine as well.'

'But still, you'd let me buy it for you as a wedding present, wouldn't you?'

Her eyes remained fixed on the scarf, and she appeared to be imagining how well it would look on her. So once again he asked, 'Wouldn't you like to have it?'

'Oh, yes,' she answered him, 'I'd like fine to have it, but not because it's so beautiful and much too grand for me, but because it's you who's giving it to me and it would be your present to me.'

So they entered the shop. The shopman took the scarf out of the window and allowed them to see the full play of its colours. They did not dare to take it in their hands, but when they finally stroked it with infinite caution, they were amazed by the frail delicacy of the material.

Then the shopman said, 'I can let you have it for only thirty marks.' And they both felt embarrassed because Karl had only five marks on him, itself a quite considerable sum in view of his modest income. But when he saw the longing which lit up the face of his girl, he came to an arrangement with the shopman whereby the scarf would be laid on one side, and Karl would bring him six marks every second week until it had been paid for.

What happiness they knew as they went into town every second Sunday to hand over the small sum of money and gaze at the scarf in the window for half an hour; since it was his most expensive item, the shopman had put it back on display.

When they came together in the evening after the heavy labour of the day, they never tired of picturing in their minds, without many words passing between them, the pleasure that they would have from this splendid scarf for the rest of their lives. In the end, every measure of the longing which their simple hearts possessed was focussed on the scarf. Unconsciously they both sensed it to be a symbol of fulfilment.

And gradually it came to be a bond of such strength between them that the common spiritual interests of more complicated natures could not have united them more closely.

Then at last the Sunday arrived when the shopman wrapped it for them in fine blue tissue paper and placed it in an elegant cardboard box which alone seemed worth the price to them. In the afternoon they went to the dance, but not for long; then they strolled through the village, so that all might see her treasure. She drew happiness from every admiring look, each astonished glance that followed her. Towards evening they left the village and walked through the fields over bank and stile. When night had fallen, the scarf became their sweet bridal cloth. They bathed in depths of pure joy.

And because they did not return home until late into the night, they had not heard a whisper of what had happened. Karl had to leave only two days later. They did not grieve, for they never doubted but that whatever happened was meant to be and could not be helped. Karl had worked for the first half of the day, but then he said to the farmer, 'That's enough now, I want the rest of the day completely to myself.'

Then he went to his girl and said to her, 'Look, Klara, I think I'll make you a fine wooden box with a strong lock on it; then you can always put your beautiful scarf in it, and all the letters I'll be writing you. Not that I'll be away for very long. Nowadays a war only lasts for three or four months at most.'

She simply nodded and sat quietly watching him construct the box and then decorate it beautifully with roses and forget-me-nots. When the little chest was finished at last, she exclaimed over and again, 'Oh, that's such a wonderful thing you've made!'

Then she laid the scarf carefully inside it, as though she were handling a fragile ornament.

'That's the treasure chest,' he said with a smile.

She wanted to return his smile, but felt the tears start from her eyes and bent quickly over the scarf, as if to arrange it more smoothly and tidily.

He wrote to her often enough. But she was unable to respond to the letters with the personal warmth that comes so easily to more educated people. Each Sunday, however, when her work was done, she would shut herself in her room, open the wooden box, and unfold the scarf. She pressed it to her lips before spreading it out, and kissed it again before she locked it away. It was only the scarf that brought her close to him. She would imagine that she could feel his breath in the fine silk threads and see his good-humored, merry eyes in the sheen of the material. Never again did she wear it outside her room, once he had gone away.

Late in the autumn she heard that he had been killed; and into her thoughts she wove the stubborn notion that everything he had been as a person was now absorbed into the scarf. At about this time the farmer's wife lost one of her rings, a circumstance which put it into her mind that many other things had also been disappearing recently. No doubt the missing objects were to be found in the wooden box which the servant cherished like a sacrament. When this suspicion arose, Klara was on her way into town to run an errand for the farmer.

'Well, what are we standing about for?' the farmer's wife said to her husband. 'Why should we wait until she comes back and hides everything away? I'd like to know who in the world can stop me from looking around my own house to see what's tucked away in bags and boxes.'

So the farmer went into the servant's room and broke open the box. And because it was really strong and solidly made, the beautiful red roses and forget-me-nots and the smooth-planed edges were spoilt beyond repair. But none of the missing objects were found.

When the girl returned home that evening, she found the splintered box and beside it the silk scarf, crumpled and torn by the farmer's muddy boots. With inexpressible tenderness she picked up the scarf and pressed it to her face, and when she had folded it and laid it on her lap, then saw before her the fractured tendrils of the roses, she wept impassioned tears, the tears she had not wept when he went away, had not wept when she heard that he would not return.

The insurance on the farmer's hay-filled barn was not due to come into effect until the following day, but that night it burned to the ground. The girl had done nothing to shield herself from suspicion.

'And,' as the state prosecutor said some time later, 'what betrays a quite exceptional villainy on the part of the culprit, what can only nip in the bud any extenuating circumstance in her favour, is that she perpetuated this wicked act, an act which in present conditions might even be called unpatriotic, on account of a paltry shred of silk and an unremarkable wooden box.'

The members of the court and the entire public gallery applauded these sensible and lucid arguments.

The Actor and the King

It seldom happens.

Fortunately.

Yet once it did occur that an actor chose a king to be his friend.

Or perhaps it was the other way round.

But in the end it makes no difference.

The two of them were honest and sincere friends. They quarrelled and were reconciled, as is generally the custom between true friends.

For two years their friendship held.

The actor made no more ado about this friendship than he would have done about a friendship with any other mortal.

One afternoon they went strolling together in the park.

The actor had played a king the evening before. But not a Shakespearean king. The royal patron of the theatre could not endure those. For Shakespeare's kings, notwithstanding their divine right, were quite ordinary men who loved and hated, murdered and reigned—just as it suited their intents and purposes.

The part of the king in the play of the previous evening, however, had been written by an author who was an anarchist at the age of eighteen, though later he was appointed a privy councillor.

It is understandable that this part should have delighted the king enormously and gave him occasion to converse with the actor on the problem of representing kings on the stage.

'What is the sensation you encounter, dear friend, when you appear in the role of a king?'

'I feel myself to be totally a king, with the result that I would be incapable of any gesture which does not suit the character of a king.'

'That I can understand very well. The crowd of extras, bowing before you as the stage directions instruct them to do, sustains your sense of majestic dignity and suggests to the audience that you are indeed a king.'

'Even without the supporting actors I remain a king in the eyes of my audience—even if it should happen that I must be quite alone on stage and deliver a monologue!'

This magnificently artistic conception of the actor's stimulated the king to draw a strictly circumscribed comparison between himself and the thespian king.

'But nonetheless, there remains an unbridgeable abyss between a real king and a theatrical king. However remarkable your performance as a king, you cease to be a king as soon as the curtain descends. Suggestibility and dramatic illusion put an end to your majesty as soon as they cease to operate. Whereas I, my dear fellow, I remain a king even when I lie in my bed!'

To this the actor rejoined, 'My dear friend, your comparison applies to both of us. No more than a short while ago we drove in a carriage to the gates of this park. Countless people lined the streets or ran behind us. They waved—you returned their greeting. They shouted as loud as they had breath, "Long live the King!" and "Hurrah!"—you smiled. Rather smugly. But if these people should ever cease to play their parts as unpaid extras, then you also—and not only in your bed, but also in the clear light of day—you also, my friend, will cease to be a real king!'

The king halted abruptly in his tracks.

He stared fixedly at the actor.

His lips grew pale and began to quiver.

Suddenly he turned on his heel.

Briskly he walked to the carriage and rode home.

Alone.

The friendship was at an end.

The friends never saw one another again.

And never again did the king attend the theater.

He became a thinker.

Became obsessed by the notion that he was a quite ordinary mortal.

Consequently had to abdicate.

Died five years later.

His mind deranged.

It was said.

A Writer of
Serpentine Shrewdness

Suspecting no evil, I was sauntering through the backstreets of
the town. Then, sudden as the legendary bolt from the blue, the
noted writer Bogumil Scheibenkleber came rushing at me, ges-
turing wildly in that inimitable matter so natural to him, and
yelled into my face, 'Splendid fellow! How fantastic to bump into
you like this! I've done it! The absolute masterpiece of all time!
It's terrific! Gigantic! Stupendous!'

'What's up?' I asked innocently.

'Lots of cash!'

'You don't say?'

'No, seriously. It's a novel.'

'Not that again!'

'Eh?'

'I mean: again so soon?'

'But this time it can't fail, I tell you. We'll be simply splashing
about in coin of the realm.' With that he handed me a sheet of
paper torn from a notepad and covered in writing on one side,
adding triumphantly, with invincible self-assurance, 'Just read that!'

On other occasions when we had been out walking together,
he would turn to look at every woman we passed and would

make remarks, inoffensive or otherwise, about her, or sometimes would stop quite tactlessly in order to stare after her in the most conspicuous manner. That day, however, his eyes did not leave my face for a moment, and so intense was the enthusiasm he felt for his own work that he flung his arms and legs about excitedly. In the meantime I was reading the scrap of paper with interest:

* * * * * *

The Transgressions of the Apothecary's Young Wife A Novel in Three Parts by Bogumil Scheibenkleber Part 1, Chapter 1: A small town. Chapter 2: Rosa is the strikingly beautiful and passionate wife of the apothecary; her husband Wagemut is the hard-working and ambitious owner of the dispensary. Chapter 3: She is fabulously sophisticated. Chapter 4: Frightfully proud. Chapter 5: Unrequited longings in her heart and so forth . . .

In this fashion the contents of the novel had been sketched out in three volumes and thirty-six chapters. Chapter 35 was entitled:

Yet in the end the priest gave way, for the doctor had diagnosed melancholy. Chapter 36: The funeral was wonderful.
The End

* * * * * *

Apart from the title and the above-mentioned headings there was nothing on the piece of paper.
I handed it back to Bogumil. But when he saw from my puzzled

frown that I was on the point of making some comment, he intercepted my unspoken remark with a wave of his hand and said, 'Hush! Hush! Later! Later!'

Nevertheless, I was unable to suppress my opinion and said, 'The outline looks all right.'

Bogumil regarded me sympathetically and replied, 'What's that you say? Outline? Out...line? Oh, you must be demented. Come on, you're about to get the shock of your life.' And with that he hustled me into the shop of Rispenhalm the bookseller, who published most of his work, and bore down upon the latter's private office, carrying me in his wake. He flung the door open with an inspired flourish and cried, with darting gestures, 'Great news! Terrific news! I tell you, Rispenhalm, it's worth at least a million.'

The publisher rose to his feet and gave one deep and one shallow bow. 'Ah, good day to you, Scheibenkleber,' he said. 'Is that you back again?' And shaking him cordially by the hand, he added as if by way of an aside, 'Well now, what is it that you have for me this time? Here, do have one of these. An excellent brand.'

Saying which he pushed a crystal cigarette box over to Bogumil.

With impressive sleight of hand Bogumil tossed a cigarette into the air and caught it between his lips, whereupon he said, 'A novel.'

'A humorous one?' Herr Risp;enhalm enquired.

'No, tragic,' was Bogumil's reply.

'Hm!' answered Herr Rispenhalm. 'Novels can be a bit tricky sometimes, you know. Sometimes they sell, sometimes they don't. Now if you had some hypermodern poems or something—'

'But look, when I brought you my metropolitan lyrics six months ago, what was it you said then?'

'What did I say, he asks. Heavens, what haven't I said at one time or another. And after all, I did publish them, you know, so what more do you want?'

'Maybe, but you paid me nothing for them.'

'Why so impolite all of a sudden, Bogumil, dear chap? Won't you have another cigarette? Really is the choicest blend. Now, why don't you just let me finish what I was saying. You see, Bogumil, tastes change and so—'

'Yes, tastes change, Rispenhalm, you couldn't be more right about that. Exactly what I've always been saying. And it's the quintessence of poetic art to write for the taste of the broad masses. Well, I've managed to lay my finger on this quintessence. Just that: the essence, or should we say: the extract. I can assure you, it's worth a million in sales.'

'Out with it, then.'

Bogumil Scheibenkleber took the sheet of notepaper from his wallet, gave it to the publisher, lit another cigarette, and then sank confidently into the armchair.

After reading through it, Rispenhalm made as if to hand the paper back. But first he weighed it in his hands a few more times and then said, 'Yes, I think there might be something in that. The idea isn't too bad at all. If you can make a good job of writing it up, we may have a bestseller on our hands. When were you thinking to have it finished?'

Impelled from his comfortable seat by sheer astonishment, Bogumil declared in tones of unfeigned surprise, 'I don't understand what you're getting at, sir! Truly I do not. You keep on about "writing it up" and "having it finished" and so forth. Well, for heaven's sake, *what* am I supposed to finish?'

'What a question! Why, the novel of course.'

'But good God, it *is* finished.'

'Oh, I see! Why couldn't you say so right away? Then just drop it in to me.'

'What d'you mean, drop it in? Drop *what* in, for goodness' sake?'

'Have I really gone mad? I want you to bring me the completed novel.'

'My dear Rispenhalm, will you please stop monkeying around! You're holding it in your hand at this very moment.'

'What?'

'The completed novel.'

Rispenhalm first blinked his eyes, then looked at me, then at Bogumil, then he chuckled and finally advanced on Bogumil with his index finger raised, tapped him on the forehead, and said paternally, 'Bogumil, dear fellow, have we been seeing a bit too much of the high life these past few nights, eh? Or maybe it's the ladies? Steady, Bogumil, steady, don't overdo it! Hee, hee, hee, hee.'

'Will you please stop giggling like some damned moron!' Bogumil was enraged. 'I'm in dead earnest. Tell me, do you intend to accept my novel or do you not? If you won't publish it, I can tell you right now that you're...that you have not the vaguest notion of how to run your business. It's a sad state of affairs when an honest man of German letters has to come along and show you how before you're capable of running your business and turning a profit.'

'But I thought—'

'Then stop thinking and do something for a change! Don't you come to me any more with your overbearing self-importance and try to make out that you're a publisher who keeps up with the times. You haven't the slightest notion of what troubled times you live in and what they need so badly. It really is the most appalling scandal.'

'Isn't it about time that you explained yourself more clearly?'

'What is there that needs explanation? We live in the age of the punch line, the aphorism, the three-line joke, the seven-line story, and that's including the title and the author's name. I suppose that even you must know that. After all, you do read the newspapers.'

'Indeed I do, and they have the ring of truth.'

Bogumil seized Herr Rispenhalm by the arm and marched him around the room, lecturing him all the while on his latest intellectual acquisition: '...so the shorter a work of literature happens to be, the more valuable it is. The reader of today will measure the written word in gold, as long as the proper amount of skill has been brought to the task of stringing together as few words as possible and making it appear that they are the crystallised manifestations of the most divinely inspired sparks of genius. What's most valuable of all has to be written between the lines. Now pay attention, I want you to publish the three volumes of my novel in a deluxe edition.'

'Stop, stop, we haven't got as far as that yet!'

'Of course we have, we're much further on than you think. So

use only the finest materials. The novel contains two hundred
and forty-nine words. More than sufficient. Any more and it
would suffer. Now, in order to underscore heavily the exhorbi-
tantly high cost of each single word, every one will have a page
to itself.'

'But, Bogumil—'

'Hush, I'm talking. Now it's impossible for the modern reader,
and we don't have to worry about any other kind, to take in bulky
novels, since he has to expend every ounce of his nervous energy
on earning his living and only on earning his living. But he needs
to have first-hand knowledge of the latest currents in literature if
he is not to fall behind the times. And beyond that he also wants
to be entertained. So by placing only one pricelessly poetic word
on each page—fabulously high-class paper, of course—we
enable the reader to turn the page without interruption. This un-
interrupted turning of the page is relaxation and refreshment for
his fatigued brain. It simultaneously excites and entertains him
in the most enjoyable fashion. That's all he asks from a writer. He
knows all the rest himself, and knows it much better, too. There
is positively far too much chatter in novels, and the same goes for
the theatre. Action—like at the cinema—that's what people
want today. They want everything they see and consume to be
unvarnished, short, terse, penetrating. They already know the
whys and wherefores only too well, and if they don't know them,
they can work it out for themselves, and if they can't work it out
for themselves, then they know how to put up with the loss and
suffer in silence. So just one word on each page. Exactly in the
middle. Above and below, right and left, leave a blank space
which cries out: Dear and gentle reader, so highly do I rate your
intelligence, wit, and artistic sensitivity that I leave you to fill in
the blanks yourself, knowing that you will do so better than my
poor scribbler's soul could ever be capable of! Do you really
believe, Rispenhalm, that our readers will not value this display
of confidence in their ingenuity? That they will not pay gladly
with solid, shining gold for the high opinion we have of them
and are letting them have in writing by offering them this book?
At ten pfennigs a word—astoundingly cheap, by the way—and
with the reader getting nine words for free, as will be emphatically

stressed in the prospectus and the advance copies, that would make it twenty-four marks for the novel, eight marks the volume.'

'That would be about the average price for a normal novel.'

'There you are then!'

Rispenhalm had been following Bogumil's exacting explanations with great interest. He seemed almost to be acquiring faith in the undertaking. But not wanting to appear devoid of wit, he therefore turned to Bogumil and said with an ironic smile, 'My dear Bogumil, I can guarantee you that in six weeks we'll have moved eight thousand copies.'

Bogumil chose to overlook the irony and said earnestly, 'Maybe eight thousand is a bit much, but if I'm any judge of the public we should manage to get rid of upwards of five thousand in eight weeks.'

'All right then,' Herr Rispenhalm retorted sarcastically, 'I'll get them to make a start on the first ten thousand right away, so we won't be in a mess if the novel should happen to sell out within a fortnight.'

The novel was published.

It really was.

Rispenhalm had taken the gamble.

But both of them, Rispenhalm as well as Bogumil, had miscalculated badly. For by the sixth week they had sold not eight thousand, as Rispenhalm had prophesied ironically, but twenty-five thousand, which disappeared like wildfire.

The BLue-Speckled SParroW

There was once an impresario.

He had the services of a competent director and a troupe of outstanding artistes.

With the commendable assistance of the director and the gracious—and contractually regulated—collaboration of his versatile troupe of artistes, the impresario succeeded, to his immense astonishment, in staging a production of such virtuosity that even the uninitiated deigned not to withold from the performance their admiration and highest respect.

It so happened that on the very same day Rooster had been inspecting a regiment of the line and was garrisoned in the town.

Rooster—for the benefit of those who may perhaps be unaware of it—was the reigning monarch, His Royal Highness the Grand Duke Joachim Horits.

Now because the Equerry of the Chamber Dexter had departed to take the waters, of which he was sorely in need, Rooster had found himself compelled, much to his distress, to bring along with him the other Equerry, he of the Chamber Sinister. This was a man of horrendous ineptitude. In consequence of a mental defect which could be traced back to the long line of his ancestors and the strictly maintained purity of his pedigree, he possessed not the slightest sensitivity to the hidden but none-theless pressing desires, large and small, general and particular, of his illustrious sovereign. He was therefore ignorant of the need for compliance, remaining unmoved by even the most frenzied wink of an eye. And hence he showed no talent for pro-curing the appropriate remedy and thus attending in a satisfactory manner, with great decorum and exquisite tact, to the royal needs.

And in his excess of boredom Rooster was put in mind of the fine arts.

In his pursuance of this majestic duty he visited the theatre.

Despite his truly outstanding knowledge of the drama and his highly cultivated artistic taste and aesthetic delicacy, he found it all simply splendid; and because the evening passed off pleasantly in other respects as well, and reached a thoroughly satisfying conclusion, he invested the impresario with the much coveted but seldom conferred Noble Order of the BLue-Speckled SParroW, in recognition of his services to 'the fine arts and liberal scholarship'.

Now whether the impresario was instantaneously struck down by delusions of grandeur, or was incapable of summoning the required measure of humblest devotion and deepest submission and respect, or was prevented by some incurable vulgarity of spirit from appreciating the inspirational delights to be derived from this lump of serrated gilt, will remain eternally beyond the bounds of human understanding. For who can fathom the tor-tuous reasonings of an impresario intoxicated with success? But what the man did now was hitherto unrivalled in its extreme eccentricity and is unlikely to happen again in the near future. May heaven forfend! For otherwise . . .

On the day after he received the Noble Order, the impresario had a six-inch nail hammered thunderously through the re-hearsals board, and from it he suspended the Order by its topaz-yellow ribbon. In order to dispel any suspicion of lese majesty and so to avoid the forfeiture of those moral qualifications deemed essential to the running of a theatre, he had the following announcement posted beneath the Order:

To the Esteemed Members of My Company

Our Most Gracious Sovereign has bestowed on me the Noble Order of the BLue-Speckled SParroW with its topaz-yellow ribbon. That this rare honour has been conferred on me is due not to my efforts, but to the outstanding contribution made by yourselves, my respected friends. As a visible token of my gratitude and to make it expressly known that you are as entitled as myself to the dignity of this Order, I am displaying the Order here as a stimulus to renewed effort in the future and as a reminder of the graciousness of Our Most Noble and Most Illustrious Sovereign. May you derive as much pleasure from it, hour by hour and day by day, as I have done.

Here the Order continued to hang for quite some time.

After It had been thoroughly and sufficiently admired and examined from front and rear, from above and below, from left and right, from inside and outside, by all the members of the company, It eventually found its way into the green room. Here It served for a while as a gewgaw for actors with stage fright. Now It lay in a corner of the sofa, now under a chair, now It was pressed into service as a door stop to prevent the door from swinging shut.

So matters continued equably enough, until one evening a gentleman who was cast in the role of a government minister noticed just as he received his cue that he had not donned the requisite decoration. Without turning a hair, the actor took It, the Order, down from the lamp-standard where It had latterly been in use as a switch cord, and pinned It to his breast.

By this act the fate of the BLue-Speckled SParroW was finally and irrevocably sealed. For after the performance the actor had an assignation with a certain lady of his acquaintance. Hence he found it necessary to remove his make-up and change his clothes with some haste, and in so doing he forgot to unpin the Order. The wardrobe master, attending to the costumes on the following morning, discovered the Order and passed It to the property master. He, being a simple man who had never previously seen a genuine decoration close at hand, consequently appropriated the Order and added It to his stock.

So it was that the Order came to rest in an old cigar box, amongst all the many stage medals made of brass, tinplate, and pressed gold and silver paper.

Here It tried at first to assume airs and graces, but the proletarian inhabitants of the cigar box soon inculcated It with the necessary talent for assimilation, so that It no longer dared open its mouth and before long was leading an entirely tranquil existence.

As was only to be expected, the membership of the company changed entirely in the course of the next two years, with the result that any memory of the resplendent greatness and majesty of the Order was lost for ever. Now at last, after the many false beginnings which no true earthly immortal is spared, the Noble Order was allowed to perform an honourable and highly distinquished mission in life such as few others of its kind can hope to achieve. With no regard for personalities, It decorated crown princes, ministers of state, generals, village sextons, railway signalmen, and champion sharpshooters, all in due turn. With equal forebearance It adorned Germans, Frenchmen, Britons, Negro boxers, and Red Indian chiefs. It celebrated its greatest moment of triumph, however, as It dangled wildly from the breast or from some other noble bodily portion of the burlesque comedian who, in a farcical song-and-dance routine, acted the part of a thickset, globular, bald-headed, newly decorated rentier and former glazier. Thunderous roars of laughter rocked the house whenever the BLue-Speckled SParroW performed its clownish antics. What would the SParroW not have given to have found some way of throwing the fact of its authenticity into the faces of the audience. And then to have seen those faces as they congealed into ice, what a triumph it would have been! The gods themselves could not have concealed their envy.

Yet one evening the topaz-yellow ribbon, by now slightly reddened by specks of make-up, came untied from the breast of an actor. The Noble Order of the BLue-Speckled SParroW fell through a crevice in the trap door and down into the basement of the building. Though eagerly sought for, It was never seen again.

May It rest in peace!

It was the only one amongst the countless millions of its cousins which not only was a source of delight to all who wore It in turn, but at the same time gave even greater pleasure to those who saw It hanging from another's breast. And that all could see It displayed without being infected themselves by the poison of envy, is proof of its imperishable greatness.

To It I owe the honour of this noble epitaph.

Originality

An actor had ambitions to be famous.

But he was not succeeding.

It is far from easy to become famous. There are not a few who fail utterly, particularly if they know what they are about and if their talent and its uniqueness tower high above the average.

A pocketful of luck is the least that is required.

And artifice. Not to forget a thorough knowledge and sound appreciation of the audience.

Luck arrived one day in the shape of the producer.

'Sir, I have a part for you here. A paragon of a part, I tell you! Well, I shall say no more. This is your chance to show what you can do. Just throw yourself into it. With a part like this you're bound to make a name for yourself, if ever you're to succeed at all.'

'Fine,' said the actor, 'I'll give it a try.'

And he took the part.

Ye gods, did he not! Took it between his teeth, in fact. He played it for better or worse, better than the author had allowed for, but worse than any other actor could possibly have played it. As to the quality of his performance we shall say nothing here. For originality is the unyielding foundation of the actor's art and not—as two or three poor simpletons with outmoded attitudes continue to insist—any innate talent. The majority must know, being always right. Until tomorrow morning.

The newspapers cut him dead. Quite simply, though his was the leading role, they did not mention him at all. And this despite the fact that they lavished two whole lines on the actor whose name appeared last in the programme, he having carried the chair onto the stage. In one newspaper he even got four and a half lines, which caused the sales of this paper to outstrip those of its rivals by twenty-four copies. For there were precisely twenty-four theatrical agents to whom the chair-carrier was immediately obliged to write.

The producer said, 'Sir, you are a bitter disappointment to me. Where have you been hiding yourself? So far I have seen neither hide nor hair of you. Get out there and make something of this marvellous role.'

'I shall do my level best, sir,' said the actor, and made the role that of a cunning schemer with wildly rolling eyes, flaming red hair, and blood curdling grimaces.

The newspapers decided that they would rather wait and see.

'Sir,' the producer pronounced, 'it grieves me deeply to say this, since you personally are quite a likeable chap, but where is the profit in that for me? If you cannot make something of this part, I shall find myself compelled to reduce your salary by a third. At least.'

To which the actor replied, 'I shall do all that stands within my power.'

And for all he was worth he hurled himself into the role of a dilettante who positively reeked of unctuous magnanimity yet possessed a great deal less natural sensitivity than the dear departed millowner of the play (which took some doing).

Thereafter his colleagues took to addressing him only with the most elaborate courtesy and pursued him with secretive whisperings whenever his back was turned.

The producer sent him formal notice of the reduction in his salary and informed him verbally that if he (the actor) did not immediately make something of this magnificent part, then he (the producer) would be morally obliged in the sight of God and man to implement a further diminution (no producer would use as alien a word as 'cut' in such circumstances) of his salary by yet another third, for such—hm!—performances were to be had more cheaply elsewhere.

The actor: 'I shall apply myself to the best of my abilities.'

The part was reshaped into that of an elegantly sarcastic wit. The majority of the newspapers ignored him. Yet some were more generous. One of these mentioned the name of the character and after it printed three question marks in brackets. Another did the same, except that between the brackets it placed an exclamation mark in apostrophes. The one which employed the most waspish critic, however, walled in between the parentheses first a colon and after it a semi-colon. *That* the actor had truly not deserved.

The actresses resolved quite energetically that in future they would forbid him any intimacies.

The producer, formally in writing: '...as previously agreed, implement a diminution of the salary stipulated in your contract by a further third. Hence from the first of the coming month you will receive only...'

And verbally: 'Sir, I cannot find it within me to deprive you of yet another third. I am not, after all, such a barbarian that I would rob you of the wherewithal to obtain your crust of bread. But to safeguard the reputation of my establishment—for your acting is already driving the audiences from my doors—I must urgently request that you finally make something of this part. I myself would like the chance to earn a bit of money, instead of being a loser all the time. You arouse no interest, sir! Do you hear me? You arouse no interest, and in the theatre that is what it all comes down to in the end. What you lack is originality.'

The actor: 'I give you my most solemn promise, sir, that I shall set my heart's blood, my very soul, into it. You shall not be disappointed.'

In the first act he transformed the part into that of a sophisticated raconteur, in the second act he became some species of faun, rushing from side to side in a welter of words and phrases like a infuriated chimpanzee, in the third act he fused both characters into an indefinable composite, and in the fourth act he finally returned to his senses.

For the first time in a hundred years rotten eggs were thrown onto the stage, and there was uproar as the audience demanded the return of its hard-earned money.

The newspapers inserted three daggers after his name and in addition threatened to boycott the theatre, on the grounds that it had become a place where both life and reason were in jeopardy.

The stalls grew more deserted with each performance. Those who would otherwise have occupied them now preferred the sex and horror to be seen in the cinema, whilst the cultured amongst them booked seats for the latest operatic hit, 'The Chauffeur with Intestinal Worms'. Here they recuperated from the ennobling influence of serious plays.

The producer found the play unrecognizable, and with mulish incivility informed the actor that his engagement would be terminated forthwith if he did not put an end to this intolerable buffoonery.

The other actors and actresses consequently began to spit at his feet, and those who played opposite him took to turning their backs on him in full view of the audience.

Now the role became that of a mumbling oaf with senile dementia. The safety curtain had to be brought down to prevent innocent blood being spilled.

The producer to the actor: 'You shameless rogue, give up the part at once! Or do you intend to go on treating me like an ass because I believed in you and tolerated you for so long? Give up the part at once, then clear out! This instant! You're nothing but a public nuisance. Out with you!'

The actor from outside: '— — —'

It would be improper to repeat his comments here.

Then he went home, and with a cry of 'At least you will never take it alive!' he seized hold of the part, ripped it into innumerable shreds, and scattered it across the room.

But when it appeared that there was no one with the heroic courage needed to step into the role that evening, the prompter being as hoarse as a frog besides, he was told to play the part once more at the evening performance. For the last time.

And because it was the last time and there was no longer any reason to care one way or the other, he picked up the shreds from the floor and pieced them together at random, in whichever order they came to hand. From sheer boredom he then proceeded to learn the part as it was now assembled.

Thus he acted the role that evening. With malice aforethought.

All his fellow artistes, ladies and gentlemen alike, were thrown into utter confusion. They collided with one another like a colony of demented ants and spoke their lines as if delirious.

The backdrops were no longer suited to the action. When the summer heat was mentioned, snow lay deep on the rooftops, and when another actor was dazzled by the sun (as the script demanded), it was darkest night. It rained in the drawing room and upholstered furniture appeared in the midst of virgin forest. The curtain fell abruptly on stirring speeches and cut ruthlessly through the most meaningful dialogues. And when it was raised again, the firemen were standing about the stage and getting in the way (as they invariably do), and the stagehands were running around in their shirtsleeves, cursing and swearing (as they also invariably do). The director had to be sprinkled continuously with cold water, and the stage manager, seized with a persecutional mania, was bound with stout ropes and gagged into silence.

Like a weasel the author ran back and forth along the rows of seats, everywhere insisting that the audience should show him their programmes, because he entertained justified doubts as to whether that really was his play being performed up there.

The audience was in turmoil. Calling for the author, the producer, the director, they carried the actor down from the stage in a frenzy of jubilation and bore him round the theatre in triumphant procession.

After the performance the actor was offered standard contracts with the most handsome terms by twenty-four agents and twelve theatrical producers. But his producer promised to raise his salary tenfold and have him declared in breach of contract if he accepted any one of their offers.

'You see,' he added with elaborate courtesy, 'I always told you there was real meat in that part. All you had to do was make something of it. As indeed I knew you could. So why not right from the start? Originality is the ticket. Doing something special. Something that's not been done before. It doesn't have to be right. We can safely leave such tomfoolery to the provinces. You'll come and join me for a few bottles of bubbly this evening, hm?'

The other actors swept off their hats in his presence and from sheer veneration no longer dared to address him. And that business about keeping his distance, said his female colleagues, they hadn't meant it like *that*, no, they had meant something entirely different. Rather the opposite, if they might explain. But being so refined, he had simply misunderstood.

The newspapers wrote that he seemed to be improving. It would be premature to discount the possibility that he might yet amount to something, given sufficient dedication and further evolution of his originality.

But one critic, not lacking in temperament, but being very young and inexperienced and consequently not in a position to have acquired sufficient familiarity with the inner workings of a well-ordered metropolitan theatre and with the artistic preferences and whims of that great arbiter of taste, the theatre-going public, wrote: 'Mr So-and-so lost his reason completely last night. We had long been expecting it, but we did not suppose that it would happen so swiftly and painlessly.'

The actor went to see this man, shook him by the hand, and said to him, 'Sir, I have been unable to share your opinions in the past. But now I concede that you are right in every particular.'

'How so?' asked the critic. But the actor was already through the door and away. And could hear him no longer.

The critic was forced to give so much serious thought to the actor's words that in the end he found himself obliged to abandon his profession and become a fashion reporter. Young though he was, he no longer believed that there might still be honesty among artists.

The public fought pitched battles to acquire tickets.

The producer became a millionaire.

The actor bought himself a country estate.

In his own lifetime a magnificent monument was erected in honour of the actor.

Of all the thousands of people, great and small, who are

thought worthy of a memorial so that their names might be preserved for posterity, he was one of those exceptional few who had honestly deserved it.

In all seriousness.

For he best of all had discerned what the times demanded of him and what his contemporaries understood by originality.

Deceivers

Once there was a mother.

She bore a son and raised him with honour.

And she loved him greatly.

The boy wanted to play with his little friends and tumble about like his little friends. But his mother, in fear and anguish for his health and life, said to him, 'My son, stay by me. Do not leap and tumble about, for you may fall and come to harm. Do not forget that you owe eternal gratitude to your mother who gave you life.'

And her son did as she bade him and from the window looked out on the unruly games of his friends.

He grew to be eighteen and wanted to enter a profession which would have brought him great happiness. But his mother said to him, 'My son, earn money above all else, so that you may ease and enrich the existence of your mother who gave you life and to whom you owe eternal gratitude.'

And her son chose a profession which filled him with loathing yet offered him money at once.

In his twenty-eighth year he met a woman of grace and beauty. They loved each other greatly and were filled with a burning desire to possess one another.

But the mother said, 'My son, surely you have me? Am I not enough for you, that you should now cast me aside for the sake of a stranger? Never forget that you owe eternal gratitude to your mother who gave you life.'

The girl was found dead in the forest with a pistol beside her, and the son fell into melancholy. For ten years he sorrowed deeply in his heart.

In the eleventh year his colleagues came to him and offered him their friendship, until at length they took him by the arm and said, 'Dear chap, the nation stands in need of men. We must not stand idly by while others sacrifice both blood and soul to guard the precious endowments of the nation. It is base and unmanly not to rally to the flag in times of ferment. Forwards arm in arm! The prize is freedom and the flame of victory!'

But the mother said, 'My son, remember that I am your closest kin. What is the nation to you? In the pain of my flesh I gave you birth, but for me you would not have been brought into this world. So it is to me, and to me alone, that you we eternal gratitude.'

And in the fiftieth year of his life, some men came to him and said, 'Listen, you are one of the ablest men in the country. Help us, We shall carry true civilization to foreign lands and bring good works to our poor brothers. We shall shelter them from the ravages of disease, the horrors of war, the indignities of slavery.'

At this his eyes grew bright, he drew himself erect, and his resolve hardened.

But the mother said, 'My son, I am growing old. Stay by me. Do not let me die among strangers. Do not forget that you owe eternal gratitude to your mother who gave you life.'

His hair turned white and his gait became bowed and heavy.

He was begotten in a blessed hour of happy oblivion. For eighteen years his mother had clothed and fed him and raised him with devotion, because it gave her pleasure without equal to watch him grow and to rejoice in him. In return he had sacrificed to her sixty years of abstention and denial.

But as she lay dying, she took him by the hand, drew him close to her, and said as she shuddered with the horror of death, 'Oh my beloved son, why cannot I take you with me, that you might be a support to me if I should ever stumble on this dark and heavy path? Why not? Alas, why not? It was I who suffered the pain of giving you life, and therefore you owe me eternal gratitude. That you must never forget, my son, for as long as you live.'

On the very day of the funeral he collapsed as he stood by her coffin and died of heart failure an hour later. In his pocket he carried a vial of prussic acid, in case events had taken a different turn.

They were laid side by side in a common grave.

Of all the mothers who followed them on their final journey—and there were many—not one of them would have hesitated to present this 'faithful son' to their children as an example most worthy of emulation.

When a schoolmaster learned of the story, he recorded it word for word and gave it a pre-eminent position in the primary reader for the lower and intermediate forms.

A mother, a son, a schoolmaster.

Three meritorious people, one of whom is definitely a deceiver.

Or all three.

For they cheated life of the best it has to offer.

Although each of them acted with impeccable integrity and did his duty most faithfully.

More faithfully than might reasonably have been expected.

Titles

His father had started out by hawking cigars, pipe tobacco, and snuff around the villages. Later he died a millionaire and the owner of great factories. His son attained the rank of Commercial Counsellor. Primarily for no other reason than that, as the heir of his father, he was a millionaire and factory owner from the outset. In other respects he had done nothing to deserve the title.

This son spent January and February in Egypt, March and April on the Riviera, May in Biarritz, June and July in Trouville, and August, by way of recuperation, in Zoppot or Heringsdorf, or not infrequently in Norderney. Even so, strange to relate, work in the factories went at a steady pace, so that if anyone had actually bothered to think seriously about the matter, it could only have come as something of a surprise that such a thing was possible. Then in September he returned home to be received like a reigning monarch by the mayor and town council, not forgetting the other dignitaries of the little town. From October to Christmas he did a spot of work, before returning to Egypt again in January. It was this nerve-shattering programme which had enabled the Counsellor to increase his private fortune to four millions in the space of ten years, and to augment his other holdings by three new factories.

There was reason enough to suppose that the Counsellor might have been content. But money is not everything. Sad to say, in the midst of all his riches he was sorely afflicted. For it so happened that his brother-in-law, who did not possess nearly as much money, had risen even higher. He was a Privy Counsellor of Commerce. But what tipped the balance and finally persuaded him that his social position was no longer sufficiently elevated was that a humble machine manufacturer of the town had also been made a Commercial Counsellor only a short time before.

In spite of this presumed discrimination, the Counsellor had nevertheless remained a good Christian and an even better patriot. The National-Liberal election funds owed many a hefty donation to his generosity, and his voluntary contributions to the Navy League brought in more than those of all the other members put together. Admittedly, there were whose who argued that he, as one of the major consumers of tobacco, had a solid material interest in the strength of the Fleet. But that was certainly no more than malicious gossip, for in reality his actions were motivated solely by the purest patriotism. Had this not been the case, His Royal Highness the Prince Christian would surely not have stayed as a guest in the home of the Counsellor when he honoured the town with a visit in order to represent the Royal House at the four-hundredth anniversary celebration.

The Prince had remained in residence for upwards of a month, but still the Counsellor had not got his title. All that his generous hospitality had brought him was a decoration of the Second Class. By chance the mayor had also been awarded the same decoration, a state of affairs which the Counsellor secretly regarded as a deliberate insult to his person.

He just had to become a Privy Counsellor. And without delay. What was the point of having all the money otherwise? It was a cause only slightly more dear to him than to his wife, who would willingly have given her soul to be the consort of a Privy Counsellor. Who could say, the next step might even have been a peerage. And why not indeed!?

The Counsellor's lady was young and extremely beautiful, a woman of noble bearing with the polished manners of an aristo-crat. Merciful heavens, surely her husband could lay his hands on a title? There was everyone thinking she must be a countess at least, and to be no more than the wife of an ordinary Counsellor, the same as any run-of-the-mill Court butcher's wife who'd probably not been above stuffing the sausages herself—never! And again never!

Sometimes in Cairo or Nice or even in Trouville, as the young beaus swarmed about her and addressed her as 'Baroness', she almost died of shame at the thought that her husband was a mere Counsellor. All of them, on hearing the phrase 'Counsellor's lady', would have been reminded irresistibly of some dignified old dame long past her prime. Indeed, it was all very embarrassing. For she attracted a great many admirers. Almost too many, her husband sometimes thought. Though of course she was still only thirty and her slim and elegant figure made her look even younger. Not that the Counsellor himself was in his dotage. Forty-five, perhaps, and with very little of that self-satisfied dignity associated with Commercial Counsellors. So who would be such a misanthrope as to think badly of this charming young couple for aspiring to a high-sounding title?

The Counsellor was a charitable man. Despite his wealth. A rare occurrence indeed. But he was known for it both far and wide. Whenever the Counsellor subscribed a hundred and fifty marks to the paupers' hospital, two hundred marks to the orphans, five hundred marks to the missionaries, it was always reported in the local paper. Poor people who wrote to him or called at his door to ask for assistance seldom received anything. But he could hardly be expected to give to all and sundry, and then, each New Year's the newspaper was able to report that the Counsellor had paid two thousand marks into the poor box. But the 'people', it would appear, can never cram enough down their throats. Moreover, there was the annual distribution of Christmas gifts, fully reported in the paper's local columns. No, even the most poisonously envious would have to concede that here was a true benefactor of humanity who showed heartfelt sympathy for the plight of the poor and the needy. Even the metropolitan newspapers had occasion to mention the Counsellor from time to time, if he had handed over some large sum to the town or to some charitable foundation. At all events the town had every reason to be proud of him. And one fine day the town council, on the motion of the mayor, resolved unanimously—yes, unanimously, you dogs in the manger—that the Counsellor should be made a freeman of the town. These tidings were greeted with rejoicing on every hand. At the expense of the Counsellor, his workers were treated to a splendid banquet with dancing to follow, during which the Counsellor himself took the floor with the wife of a maker of cigar wrappers, while his gracious lady danced with a humble sorter, as was recorded in bold type in the following day's paper, thus leaving free reign for the practised reader to draw the usual conclusions about 'wondrous harmony' and the like, whereby the intended purpose was in fact attained. It was quite unreasonable to take offence because the Counsellor did not pay out any wages for that day, though it was enough to transport the type of ne'er-do-well wno is never happy unless he has something to grumble about into a towering rage. It was not as if any work had been done that day. Besides, the workers had been given a good feed, and every last one of them had received the equivalent of ten marks in beer. But with their depressingly familiar loutish greed, and their total misrepresentation of the imaginary consequences of such factory festivities, there is simply no satisfying these people. Not that anything can be done about it; one can only resign oneself to it with philosophical composure and not lose faith in the eternal truth of human goodness.

Naturally, the occasion was also celebrated with appropriate festivities in the mansion of the honorary freeman. But while the evening began in stately splendour, it ended on a note of shrill disharmony. A political disagreement led to a heated exchange between the Senator and his host. And the two of them parted in bitter enmity, a most regrettable circumstance. As he entered the bedroom with his lady wife, the Counsellor gave voice to the portentous utterance, 'I can manage without that ape and his filthy weed of a mug. He can go to hell.' A thoroughly unseemly and highly disrespectful remark to make about the leading governmental plenipotentiary of the district. But it was forgivable in comparison with the derogatory utterance voiced by the Senator:

'Now that repulsive oaf can wait for his title until he turns blue in the face. Conceited jackanapes!' It will be noted from both of these utterances that the two gentlemen had chosen to dispense with the formalities of mutual esteem. And that could only bode ill for the State.

His appointment to honorary citizenship received equal prominence in the newspapers of the capital city of the Empire. But still no word of the title.

Hope springs eternal in the human breast. Thus it happened that the Counsellor endowed the Lutheran church in his native town with an enormous pair of beautifully executed windows, and the Catholic church—since there was no telling which religion was momentarily the more highly prized in the leading circles of society—with a richly ornamented communion cup and two costly altar cloths. And to dispel any jealousy on the part of the townspeople, he built a gymnasium and presented it to the town. When it was due to be inaugurated, he happened to have just returned from his seaside resort. And as if they had been waiting only for his return, a deputation from his work force appeared two days later and requested an audience with him, which he most loyally granted. The deputation urged the Counsellor to install bathing facilities in the factory, or at least a shower bath for the men and one for the women, in view of the unsanitary working conditions. The Counsellor was most amiable, but declared himself absolutely unable to concede the necessity for such a bath house. They had managed well enough without one for the past thirty years, so why now all of a sudden? Besides, such facilities would be prohibitively expensive, and just at the moment, what with the failure of the tobacco harvest and taxes rising all the time, the market was in a damned shaky state indeed. He would be able to install a bath house only if the piece rates were reduced, and he did not want that to happen and they, the workpeople, did not want that to happen either. In the end the deputation was brought round to his point of view and made its departure.

From that moment on, however, the idea of a public bath rumbled about in the Counsellor's mind. Six months later he

built a bathhouse with a large swimming pool on publicly owned
land and presented it to the town with a not ungenerously apportioned sum of working capital.

Yet every righteous man must suffer many blows. There is too
much wickedness in the hearts of men. They see nothing but evil
in all the actions of their fellows, be the motives that prompt
them ever so noble, and believe every gesture however generous
to be an excrescence of the crassest egotism. So, too, in this
instance, unhappily. If only such wicked creatures could know
how basely they demean themselves with their petty-minded
interpretations, but then this species of semianthropoid has not
the least conception of how to comport itself with human dignity.
In the event, these vampires with human countenances claimed
in all seriousness, through mephistophelean smiles, that 'the
only reason our honorary freeman was being so generous to the
town and the churches was that he wanted to be made a Privy
Counsellor eventually. He was throwing a sprat to catch a whale.'

Oh, with what fervent desire would I gladly stop for ever the
slavering calumnious mouths of these despicable traducers
whose insolent conduct so threatens the public weal, so that
never again might their bawlings betray the utter depravity of
their mental condition. Just how wrong they were can probably
best be seen from the fact that the Counsellor did not receive
a title.

The clergy of both persuasions, as fully acquainted as any
urchin of the streets with the Counsellor's most ardent desire,
had quite confidentially communicated with the Consistory on
this matter. It in turn, in conjunction with the Mayor and Town
Council, had approached the Ministry. The Ministry took action.
But before proceeding any further, it took the precaution of
consulting the Senator, who replied in confidence, 'Your Excellency, I am unaware of any public-spirited gesture undertaken
by the said Counsellor in these parts which could give occasion
for such a distinction to be conferred on him. That he does rather
more than many others in the locality is—in view of his private
means, and disregarding entirely any associated and perhaps
intentional advertisement of his products—not such a service as
would allow his appointment to the rank of Privy Counsellor to

appear in any way justified.' That satisfied the Ministry to perfection.

The world ambled on in the same old way. The Counsellor departed on his travels, returned in the autumn to do a spot of work, and departed on his travels again.

The baths flourished and prospered. One of the church windows was demolished by a satanic thunderbolt and replaced at the Counsellor's expense, while the altar cloth in the Catholic church began to show signs of being stained with candle wax. Then it came to pass that the Senator, playing *vingt-et-un* in the convivial company of several officers who were garrisoned in the county town, lost the paltry sum of twenty-five thousand marks in promissory notes in a single night. Being still very young and having before him a brilliant career which he had no desire to renounce, the Senator considered himself too indispensable to have immediate recourse to the revolver. Alas, there was nothing for it but to swallow the bitter pill! He wrote confessing his bad luck at cards to the Counsellor, who just then was in Nice. By return the Senator received from the Counsellor a letter which contrived to include the following passage: '... in which connection I am put in mind of a certain "confidential" enquiry addressed to Your Excellency.' So the fellow had got wind of it and consequently there was nothing doing in that quarter. A bitter pill indeed. But as the Senator set about composing his letter of resignation, he was handed a message saying that a benefactor 'who wished to remain anonymous' had transferred twenty-five thousand marks to the Senator's account, which he might use as he saw fit. The cheque was signed in the Counsellor's name. And so a delighted Senator wrote to a forgiving Counsellor to say that he would now like to perform some small service in return, so that matters, whose felicitous outcome he could guarantee, might soon be brought to a conclusion. The Counsellor, not wishing to let it be said that he was miserly, sent one hundred thousand marks to the county treasurer for the building of a district hospital.

From the Ministry, however, the Senator received the following decision on his petition: 'The contradictory reports which we have received on the charitable activities of the said Counsellor here recommended for elevation in rank have given cause for doubt in authoritative circles as to the propriety of petitioning for the title to be conferred at the present time. Moreover, such has been the excessive use made in the preceding year of elevation to and conferral of the distinction of Privy Counsellor, that following an audience granted to His Excellency by His Majesty the quite specific wish was expressed that further conferral of this distinction should be withheld unreservedly for the foreseeable future.'

It was the Senator himself who travelled the weary road to Nice and acquainted the Counsellor with these sad tidings. They were accepted by their recipient with remarkable fortitude. There was indeed nothing that could be done...

In the bedroom that evening he and his wife reckoned up how much he had already spent on the title. The total was two hundred and eighty-five thousand marks. And the most disgusting part of it was that so far he had got nowhere. Resignedly, he subsided onto the divan and said, 'It's just not meant to happen.' But then his listlessness was thrust aside by a savage vigour: 'No, I want it now. Even if I have to fork out a million. I want it now!'

But the Counsellor's good lady, who was already undressed, said merely, 'You are a hippopotamus. You're not to spend another pfennig. It's high time I took matters in hand myself!'

'You?'

'Yes, me. Now if you don't mind, I'd like to get some sleep. I'm worn out.'

For the remainder of the night he puzzled over what it was that she could possibly have it in mind to do. But nothing occurred to him.

In the event she really did take matters into her own hands.

On this occasion they remained rather longer that usual on the Riviera. Then, as soon as the season opened, they departed at once for the unaccustomed pastures of Baden-Baden. There they took rooms in the Hotel Stephanie, and in the dining room were placed at the same table as a young gentleman whose conversation proved to be charming.. The Counsellor's lady appeared quite taken with him, in a way that only a sanctimonious Sunday-school teacher could have found offensive.

The young gentleman was simply too sweet. Elegant from top to toe, he nonetheless did not affect a monocle, which showed that he was a cavalier of the first water. An officer in the Guards, of course, and the Dragoon Guards to boot, but retired. He'd had his fill of junketings, or perhaps just found them tedious. Before taking up his commission he had been called to the bar, and was presently occupying a position in the Ministry of the Interior, where his course was set towards the highest offices of state. A scion of the nobility, his ancestors had more than enough blue blood in their veins even before the Crusades. Not to mention the large amount of money he had in the bank, the very large amount indeed. It would be foolish to deny that all of this made him exceptionally well qualified to behave elegantly, discharge the most lofty obligations of the cavalier, and carry on charming conversations.

The Counsellor's wife was to be envied. So outrageously did he flirt with her that the Counsellor, who was not a jealous man, nevertheless felt constrained not to prolong their luncheon for an unnecessary length of time. He offered his arm to his wife, thinking to take a stroll with her. The young gentleman asked if he might be permitted to accompany them. The Counsellor's lady agreed with surprising alacrity, so that the Counsellor had perforce to add his consent. But just at that moment he was handed some business telegrams which demanded his immediate attention, so that now all at once it was he who had to ask the young gentleman to accompany his wife.

And off they went.

'So, Baron, you may become a Minister of State?'

'Or perhaps the King of Kiaochow, madame.'

'Oh, you're teasing me! No, but seriously, do you have influence with the Minister?'

'Well, that rather depends. Small matters can be arranged if need be, madame.'

'Ah, small matters...'

'You say that in such a strange tone of voice, madame. Is there something you wish to have arranged? As far as I am able, I would be delighted to place myself at your disposal. Indeed, you would be doing me a service were you so inclined as to allow me the opportunity to oblige you.' With that he gave her such a meaningful look that she could not help but blush and lower her eyes.

They walked on.

At every step he thrust his stick into the gravel, while she plucked small green leaves from the bushes and held them between her teeth. And as though they were not sufficiently occupied, their thoughts raced tirelessly onwards. After some considerable time had elapsed, they began to speak of everything under the sun. Yet both of them had the definite feeling that their words were intended only to conceal thoughts which were becoming increasingly obtrusive. He was the first to give voice to his secret wonderings. He paid the most enticing compliments to her figure, her elegance, her refinement, the purity of her complexion, her magnificently tended hair. She scarcely dared to raise her eyes. He on the other hand did not avert his gaze from her person. And when she suddenly looked up, their eyes met.

She became a little flustered. But when he merely smiled gently, she composed herself and said, 'If, Baron, you were indeed to become a Minister, might I hope that my husband would be appointed a Privy Counsellor?'

'But come now, madame,' he laughed, 'that may well take quite some time.'

'Yes,' she sighed resignedly. 'So there is nothing for it but to wait.'

'But why so, madame?' he asked.

'His name has already been put forward, it's true. But the categorical wish has been expressed from above—from quite high above, if you understand me, Baron—that the distinction of Privy Counsellor is no longer to be conferred for the time being.'

'I see, I see. From above, you say? Well, if that is all that stands in the way, then—'

'Then?' she asked swiftly.

After a brief pause he said abruptly, as if seeing the light, 'Madame, what would be my reward if you were to be the wife of a Privy Counsellor within six weeks, starting from today?'

With some incredulity she answered, 'A kiss?'

'Only one?' he asked in reply.

'Well then—six.'

And oblivious of every chivalric virtue, he said, like a man driven by a sudden impulse to gamble everything on the play of one card, 'Forgive me if you will, madame, but is not that too small a price? Surely this elevation in rank is worth more to you than that?'

She was certainly taken somewhat aback by his boldness. But she grasped his meaning well enough. Moreover, it seemed to her that any better opportunity to combine pleasure with profit would be hard to imagine. Her desire to show her husband what she was capable of grew apace. Glancing sideways at her companion, surreptitiously she observed his candid face and insouciant smile as they continued their walk. She was not in love with him, but neither did she find him unattractive. He was interesting. No more than that, though. All the same, the longer she watched him, allowing herself to be impressed by his youthful suppleness of physique, by his elegant gestures, by the immaculate clothes that bore witness to his impeccable taste, the less impossible it seemed that she might satisfy the stirrings she felt within her. So she said to him, 'Baron, what guarantee could you offer me?'

'I will give you my word of honour in writing, madame, that your husband will be a Privy Counsellor within six weeks.'

'That I would find both satisfactory and reliable.'

'Thank you, madame.'

'Then, Baron, might I ask that you take out your notebook and prepare the document?'

This he did. Then, returning the notebook to his pocket, he read out the few words he had written and held out the paper. As she reached out to take it, however, he asked in a low voice, 'And the reward?'

'Whatever you wish, Baron.'

He directed a lingering glance into her eyes. She bore his scrutiny. Then he allowed his glance to fall over her, measuring her figure, then raised it again until his eyes were resting on hers once more. At the same time he asked, drawing out the words in a meaningful way, 'Whatever...I...wish...madame?'

And quickly she answered, 'Anything that you wish.' Then, as if she feared that he might perhaps misunderstand her, she repeated what she had said, emphasizing each word in turn. 'Anything...that...you...wish!'

They had turned aside onto a path which, winding its way

through the forest, climbed to the right before it disappeared into the mountains. They turned to face each other. He kissed her, giving her the paper as he did so. Then he asked, 'When?' On the Monday, she told him, her husband would depart for Mannheim and stay there until the following day. She would not be accompanying him. 'You may expect me then, Baron, at nine o'clock in the evening in your suite.'

On their return they met the Counsellor coming towards them and decided on an excursion by motor to the pleasure gardens of Favorite, where they would take tea in the open air. Thus the day passed off in perfect harmony. The Counsellor had concluded a business deal which was certain to yield him a profit of around a quarter of a million, the Counsellor's lady carried in her purse an agreement which would bring to fruition her long-cherished desire and also held out the prospect of a not unpleasant diversion, and the young Baron could permit himself the stimulating indulgence of contriving a plan by which to celebrate a particular evening and the attendant night with all possible elaboration, commensurate with the value of the favour bestowed on him.

On the Monday the Counsellor left for Mannheim according to plan. Alone! Evening came, and the clock struck nine!

The programme had remained unaltered. Everything went off faultlessly. The plan drawn up by the Baron was extended, without serious objection being raised by either of the participants, to include several most entertaining variations. So it was that adequate recompense was made for the Baron's word of honour.

The Counsellor returned.

One week later the Baron left for the capital in order to take up his new appointment.

Three weeks later the Counsellor held in his hand the document announcing that henceforth he was to have the title of Privy Counsellor.

'There, now, it was all worth it in the end,' he said to his wife as he beamed with joy.

And she replied, 'Yes, you ass, it was worth it!'

He was somewhat taken aback by her tone of voice and found himself strangely perplexed. They looked each other in the eye.

And clicking his tongue several times, as was his wont whenever one of his business ventures had arrived at a favourable conclusion, he reached into his pocket for his silver cigarette case, took out a cigarette, and pressed it gently between his fingers before lighting it with a match.

My Visit to the Writer Pguwlkschrj Rnfajbzxlquy

Suddenly there he was—the prodigious writer and innovator Pguwlkschrj Rnfajbzxquy. Quite instantaneously and unexpectedly large as life, like every true genius. Like anyone who gives early warning of an emerging talent, maybe even of a consistent sense of direction through several generations, and, in the final analysis, of hard work and perseverance, too, he was about as far removed from true genius as the most keen-scented rescue-dog in the Army Medical Corps is from its target. The evidence, against whose overwhelming force and irrefutability I would rail in vain: four hundred thousand seven hundred and forty-three commemorative articles by eight thousand two hundred and twenty-six literary historians, all predestined by fate to scour the calendar in a murderous search for every date of birth, death, marriage, and baptism; further proof: two impressive reviews in the *Schnupstrall Gazette*.

At all events, P.R. (and I hope it will not be asked of me that I should repeat this brain-corroding name in full each time it crops up, to my own vexation and that of the typesetter) P.R., then, first drew attention to himself with a brief but all the more substantial short story in *The Hypperia*, a monthly magazine familiar to all persons of refinement (and above all to its editor). I shall leave it

for others to examine whether this title derives from too frequent
a contact with the properties of hysteria. Not one single person
was able to understand this story by P.R. (I believe that I have
already remarked on my reasons for writing simply P.R.). And
because no one could understand it, because every rational person
couched his over-all appreciation of it in the two words, 'Rubbish,
rubbish!', just for that reason there were three and a quarter dozen
cognoscenti who prostrated themselves in reverence before P.R.
That three and a quarter dozen of these talent-spotting cognoscenti
still existed at all, incidentally, is better and more conclusive proof
than any statistic that the present war is neither reducing everything to ruin, nor forcing all and sundry to re-examine their beliefs.
Once the trumpet had been sounded, it followed that the better and
best magazines and newspapers gradually found themselves obliged,
with or without opposition, to publish stories, sketches, and poems
from the hand of P.R., in deference to the frequently expressed
wishes of their invariably long-standing subscribers.

Whichever publication one chose to open, it was sure to contain
something by P.R. And everyone, even the longest-continuing
subscriber, would round off the latest delight from the pen of P.R.
by saying to himself, 'Hm! Now, whether I am an ass or the critic
Gotthold Murschenbursch is an ass, that I really could not say.
There's not a word of it I can understand. In fact, I think it's the
most arrant drivel, not that I would dare say so to anyone. But if
my suspicions are correct, then most probably it is I myself who is
the most stupendous ass, which is something I never knew before
since I seem to have managed my business activities well enough
until now.'

P.R. worked hard and long. Plays by him were performed, and
were so impressive that now it was equally impossible to understand the critics, and this was judged to be emphatic confirmation
of the henceforth incontestable fact that one would have to remain
irrevocably an ass and deserved no further share in the treasure-
trove of contemporary literature.

Then there came such a flood of novels, stories, tragedies, sketches,
aphorisms, and intensely experienced poems of love and war, that
one could only be amazed at the prodigious fecundity of this poet
and intellectual giant who reigned from the infinite heights of his

unapproachable solitude. For truly he reigned in solitude. No one had ever met him face to face. In spirit he soared above the fallibilities of man as though he were transfixed. He shunned any contact with the lumpish mass, and the nimbus which enshrouded him left women and such as were innovators dangerously exposed to the suspicion that they suffered from religious mania. Some of them were removed to lunatic asylums where they still live today, supposing themselves to be flashes of P.R.'s inspiration. Let it be left to others more qualified in medical matters to give a popularized, yet nonetheless effective and intelligible, presentation of the peculiar forms and expressions assumed by the manic delusions of those who think themselves flashes of P.R.'s inspiration. My imagination is not equal to the task, and however much I were to strain it, it could only clumsily imitate the reality.

The rumour was spread one day, no one knew how or by what agency, that P.R. (and I have stated more than once why it is that I call him merely P.R.) lay sick and dying, with no one by his side to aid and comfort him, since none of his admirers would contemplate entering the annihilating aura of his majesty, which made Phoebus himself appear no more than a withered lump of base metal. But I am robust, I do not believe in P.R., and therefore I may defy his aura with impunity. Hence I was selected to travel to P.R. and convey to him in the hour of his demise the greetings and homage of the flock that wallowed in the dust at his feet, and also to stand helpfully by him in his final throes and faithfully note his last words, thus preserving them for the coming millenia. My lack of regard for P.R. being no secret, it was appreciated that no other person would command as much objectivity as myself in receiving into his care, with neither trappings nor trimmings, the final outpourings of this prodigious intellect. By means of some incomparable sleuthing, quixotic disguise, wrongful arrest as a spy, and numerous hoverings in imminent danger of death, drowning, starvation, palpitations, and forced conscription, I at length succeeded in ascertaining P.R.'s address. He lived in a wooded region far from the bustle of the cities, secluded from the curiosity of a malevolent world behind the high walls of Restingstones Manor, which lay surrounded by small, picturesque, ivy-clad cottages, each set in its own tidy garden.

The very name was comforting, and once in the vicinity of Restingstones Manor I did indeed feel wonderfully at peace with the world. 'Excuse me,' I inquired, 'is not this the residence of the writer Pguwlkschrj Rnfajbzxlquy?' 'Yes,' came the cheerful reply, 'though actually the patient's name is Paul Rubensessel.'

I assumed the sympathetic expression which is absolutely indispensable on those occasions when one hears the word 'patient' and said, 'Is his condition very grave?'

'No worse than usual. In the five years he's been here—'

'What!' I cried in agitation. 'Five—'

'Years, that's right. He was classed grade three at first, so we set him to work mending shoes since he's a trained cobbler. But then about three years ago he started writing for the newspapers and they pay him so well that now he can afford a house of his own as well as two private nurses. Indeed, he gets exactly the same privileges as Count Hegelsdorff, and his fortune runs into millions. Anyway, it's all the same to us what the patients occupy their time with, as long as it keeps them happy.'

'Yes,' I said, thoroughly confused. 'I don't understand.'

'To tell you the truth, neither do we,' said the senior physician. 'This must be a classic example of the fact that it's impossible to tell whether there aren't more lunatics out there than there are in here with us.'

'Stop, stop!' I cried. 'For heaven's sake tell me where I am!'

'In the Clinic for the Incurably Insane. Why, surely you knew that?'

'Indeed I did not. And Herr Pguschwlksch'—in my excitement I could no longer twist my tongue around that name which I had mastered so completely before—'and Herr Pguw—'

'Herr Rubensessel, you mean? He's been incurably ill for the last three years, and since then he's been a permanent inmate of the hospital. Quite harmless as long as he's allowed to write, but completely paralytic, just entering the fourth stage.'

Quite crushed, I could only stand there. The aura of P.R. had smitten me sorely.

And the doctor added, 'Surely you must have guessed from his scribblings how far gone he is, though if you still have any doubts, you need only hear him talk. Do you want to see him?'

I declined and left and returned to the faithful.

They would have done better not to have trusted to my objectivity. They may not rely on it, for I have no desire to be stoned to death and see my body flung to the dogs. Truly, neither P.R. nor the rationality of those of his fellows who live 'on the outside' are worth that much to me.

It is their own fault that it should be so.

The Art of the Painter

Centrally positioned in a broad meadow of lush green is a young girl of pleasing appearance who wears a blouse of forceful red, a knee-length skirt of sombre grey, stockings hinted at in brown, and white shoes. Under her arm she carries a wide-brimmed yellow straw hat. Somewhere a black tree bursts into the colourless sky. Wooded hills of blue with a touch of lilac are visible far in the background through vaporous wraiths of mist.

Such was the painting on which Ewald Henkeding had placed great hopes, yet which nonetheless passed from one Selection Committee to the next without being accepted by any of them. It was clear that the 'exhibition cobblers', as Ewald Henkeding termed the members of the Selection Committee in his own spiteful manner, were going far out of their way to steer clear of so powerful a talent as his. And whenever it occurred to him to go for a stroll round the gallery, the barren daubs and smudges he saw there were enough to give him a case of the Arctic shudders. Compared with these efforts, his 'Red and Grey on Green', as he called his picture, was a masterpiece of which even Rembrandt himself need not have been ashamed.

It so happened that I was acquainted with the red and grey lady on the green, and through her I met Ewald Henkeding one afternoon. Naturally he swept me off at once to see his studio, actually more of a badly furnished room than a studio, and showed me his masterpiece. Even though there was nothing particularly outstanding about it, I had to admit that he was right, inasmuch as there were pictures in the exhibition far inferior to his in richness of conception and technique. At all events I could see from his other work that he was not without talent and that he showed a great deal of courage in following his own individual and original paths.

Later, once we had become more closely acquainted, I began to feel sorry for him, because for all his assiduous efforts he was meeting with little success, none at all in fact. I would willingly have done something to help him, but first it was vital that he should have exhibited at least once, for where and how else could he hope to make his breakthrough? He deserved to move rather more into the foreground, and I was certain that even a small success would have spurred him on to step forcefully into the picture.

One day, rather early in the afternoon, we were once again making our leisurely way around the exhibition rooms. I could not help but notice that his glance was attaching itself dolefully and longingly to all the little stickers which, by announcing a sale, generally bring as much pleasure to the seller as to the buyer.

At this time of day there were scarcely any visitors in the gallery, and on every side the attendants were taking a post-luncheon snooze. Just at that moment a quite lunatic idea raced through my mind, and it did not surprise me in the least to hear Ewald Henkeding translate my idea into words by saying, 'I do believe that it would be possible to smuggle in a picture quite unmolested at this hour of the day.'

'Indeed,' said I, 'I'm sure it could be done. But what would be the point?'

On the following day my time was fully occupied. But on the day after that Ewald Henkeding asked me if I would be so kind as to keep an eye on the attendant in the next room and give a cough if he should happen to wake up.

Now why should the schemes of Ewald Henkeding have been any concern of mine? I was to keep my attention fixed on the man and cough if he woke up. No more than that. Whatever else happened was none of my business. Therefore by no stretch of the imagination could I be reckoned an accomplice. An inanimate instrument, at most, made use of by another and quite without responsibility for an act of which one was entirely ignorant.

A short while later Ewald Henkeding again appeared beside me and invited me to step into the next room. Here I saw a pretty kettle of fish. His 'Red and Grey on Green' was hanging cheekily in pride of place on the wall. It was only now, seeing it here amongst the other indifferent scraps of tediously daubed canvas, that I noticed just how crisp his 'Red and Grey' actually was. In that room it possessed a positively refreshing liveliness. It had the same beneficial effect as the death-defying somersault by which some tartly cynical wit throws a starchily somnolent social occasion into instantaneous disarray.

'And how did you manage to get the picture in here?' I enquired.

'Rolled it up, of course.'

'But what about the frame?'

'I've attached my picture to someone else's frame with a couple of strips of wood.'

'I see. And the picture that was there before? You pinched it?'

'As if I would do such a thing.'

'Then where is it?'

'On the other side. All I did was to turn the frame around. It just happened to be the right size.'

I lifted the frame slightly away from the wall and indeed saw the missing picture, now facing inwards.

'But the catalogue—' I ventured.

'Oh, that doesn't matter,' he replied cockily.

At that moment the attendant came into the room and made his way slowly towards us. I was frightened to death, but Ewald Henkeding was regarding his picture appreciatively. Now at close quarters, now from a distance, now peering through half-closed eyes, now looking through his fist as if it were a telescope. Then he turned his back on the picture and viewed it through his pocket mirror, waving his head from side to side and saying all the while, 'Hm, Hm! Tisk! Tisk! La! La!'

Then the attendant came to stand beside him and observed with a very expert air, 'Yes, ah...ha! Some very fine pictures we have here at the moment. This here portrait of the young lady in her pretty red blouse, for instance, it's my favourite picture. First thing I do when I arrive in the morning is to have a look at this lovely picture. And he's caught the green of the meadow just right. I'm from the country, you see, and I can tell you ...'

Sometimes it is not such a bad thing after all that these attendants are none too closely acquainted with the objects they are supposed to be attending to. A few days later I thought I had better take a look and see what it was that his painting actually represented. So I leafed through the catalogue until I came to Number 635, which identified his picture, and found there: 'Max Klett: "Red Poppy"'. At that point it struck me that it might be advisable to have a closer look at the picture. I went to the room where it was hanging and saw a sticker attached to the frame—sold twice.

A fine state of affairs.

While I was still standing there, wondering how it was possible for an original work of art to be sold twice over and how much Ewald Henkeding was likely to make out of it, what with the legal costs and so on, a party of visitors entered the room. Like a clutch of chickens around a broody hen, they were milling around an elderly gentleman whose manner was loud, officious, and didactic. It was not long before I discovered him to be a professor at the Academy who was delivering a lecture on aesthetics in the presence of the actual objet d'art, partly to students and partly to other interested persons. With inimitable dispassion he was 'explaining' the picture on show. Now he came to Ewald Henkeding's 'Red and Grey on Green'. With a glance at the catalogue to find his bearings, he then cast his eyes swiftly over the picture in a comprehensive overview and began the parade of his wisdom: 'The artist has entitled his work "Red Poppy". From the title itself, ladies and gentlemen, you will surmise the imaginative profundity of the outstanding master. There is not a single red poppy in the entire picture. It is precisely there that the painting displays its genius, it paramountcy. The only hint of red is in the blouse of the simple girl. And the powerful red of the blouse in conjunction with the emphatic simplicity of the figure compels the viewer to associate these in his mind with the recollection of the rich and abundant colour of the red poppy. Here we can apprehend a new and thoroughly modern tendency...'

One of the bystanders took a notebook from his pocket and began to write busily.

'A modern, long-awaited, and frequently intimated tendency: to express through art not what one sees, for that would be primitive and unpainterly, but on the contrary to express what one could and should see on being stimulated by the painting. To recapitulate: art should not represent reality with photographic fidelity, but by enlisting the aid of the stimulated intellect should render visible the nonexistent object.'

The party gazed with fervour at the Old Master and scarcely dared to breathe, so intense was their excitement. The gentleman with the notebook sprang hastily in front of him, and after introducing himself, asked if the learned professor would care to write an article on this topic for his arts magazine.

Now it is undeniably a feature of our times that people will throw themselves with abandoned avidity into whatever distinguishes itself by its eccentricity, be it ever so harebrained and grotesque. So it should occasion no surprise that the 'Red Poppy' became the centre of attention overnight and unleashed the most furious battles between protagonists and antagonists. Later, in the purely normal course of events, as was only to be expected, the true situation came to light, or rather to such light as was thrown on it by the Selection Committee. For reasons which are easily explained from the human standpoint, it decided in favour of Ewald Henkeding, whereupon Max Klett, also for reasons that are easily explicable from the human standpoint, declared himself satisfied with a generously apportioned sum of money. The signature could just as easily have been Klett as Henkeding.

But as everything in life proceeds in due and logical order, so Ewald Henkeding has since been represented more than once in every exhibition. He is the leading representative of that tendency which insists stringently that the title of a painting must bear no relation whatsoever to its visual content. That Henkedinkism will shortly have ground an already consumptive Futurism underfoot once and for all, is now—as there are examples to show—beyond the shadow of a doubt.

In the final analysis, of course, art does not exist for the benefit of the dim-witted plebs. And that means...

The Kind of Thing That Can Happen in France

Gaston Raille, who under the pseudonym of 'Moqueur' wrote the spirited gossip that had made the paper to which he contributed so very popular, was accounted one of the foremost short-story writers. No one knew better than he how to devastate the female psyche with elegance and grace. The females in question were the heroines of his stories, and therefore always incomparably beautiful, girlishly young and boyishly slim, wearing clothes of such intoxicating sophistication, of such elaborate and genteel modishness, that his readers soon found themselves becoming rather breathless. These females, naturally, were always head over heels in love with their gentleman friend or some such, as was absolutely necessary, for indeed Monsieur Raille would otherwise have been quite unable to write his wonderful stories, nor could he ever have become the pampered darling of the ladies.

But once the war broke out, there was not a publisher or magazine editor anywhere who would venture to purchase, let alone publish, his gallant and superbly rounded stories. The ladies, as they should, were preoccupied with other matters, and the newspapers showed not the slightest concern for the literary arts. Also as they should. Besides, Paris had already heard the roar of German ordnance and had become somewhat sceptical—by force of habit from days gone by—of the reports of victory issuing from the French military command. Hence the city had no time to waste on the writer Gaston Raille. As indeed was only natural.

But Gaston Raille had to write, so that he should not be forgotten entirely.

But what? And what about?

Here perhaps is the one and only point of contact shared by Germany and France at the present moment: when these two nations go to war, they do so wholeheartedly, sparing neither mind nor muscle; and anything that is unconnected with the war they disregard completely. Gaston Raille was therefore left with no alternative other than to bring the war under the mastery of his pen.

To begin with he experienced considerable difficulty in adjusting himself to this sphere of human endeavor; for in time and distance it lay far removed from his own, whose highways and byways, even the most secret, he knew more intimately than almost any other. But once the recommendation of a close friend with government connections had allowed him to accompany a convoy taking packages to the troops and to see the trenches for himself, once he had viewed genuine corpses of dead soldiers and had heard equally real German shells burst around him, then he had enough material for war stories to last him for years on end. The stringing together of thrilling yarns became such second nature to him that it was like a pleasant stroll through the scented gardens he had known in former days. With the same breathless avidity that had previously greeted his elegant and graceful romances, the public now threw itself upon his tales of the war, narrated from personal experience or from some true occurrence, knowing that it would find itself knee-deep in blood—German blood, of course—and deafened by the withering fire from the inevitable snipers—French snipers, of course—and by the chatter of machine guns, the whine of shells, the crash of hundreds of thousands of forty-two centimetre howitzers—a German weapon, of course, with the result that Joffre was able to, etc.—all of which kicked up such a hellish racket that his readers had to plunge their fingers fast into their ears, right up to the wrist, simply because they could stand the thunder of these many millions of angry guns no longer. Indeed, it happened on more than one occasion that some overexcitable reader fell out of his chair, persuaded by the writer's evocative powers that several of the shells fired simultaneously from the uncounted millions of guns had unleashed an earthquake, of which the chair that had overturned together with the reader was an outwardly visible sign.

Then one day he wrote a superlative story that made him famous. Made him famous almost solely on its own account, insofar as that was still possible. Yet there was another besides himself who was also made famous by this superlative story, another whose existence he did not even remotely suspect.

In his story he portrayed an episode in the life of a brave soldier of France who had covered himself in undying glory by an act of bravery and acumen such as had never before been recorded in the annals of history. Only a soldier of France, and no other, could have been capable of such a deed. It transpired that this brave soldier, in the course of a single night, by dint of boldness, bravery, determination, and sundry other superior qualities, had managed entirely by himself to overrun two German entrenchments, mop up four German dugouts, take prisoner three hundred and sixty-two men and nineteen officers, including two brigadiers and a regimental commander who just happened to be visiting each other, plus one major, and capture their rifles, sixteen pieces of field artillery, and twenty-four trench mortars. All alone and quite unaided. In a single night. Just so. And such a fine job had Gaston made of the retelling, such a thrilling picture had he painted, that readers in the cafes and streets cried out 'Bravo!', which was always addressed of course to the soldier who had achieved immortality by accomplishing such a tremendous feat. And more than one of those whose only reason for sitting at home to await the outcome of the war was that they could then grumble all the louder about how things should have been done to have been done properly, exclaimed in audible tones, 'If only we had another five hundred lads like that, we could finish the Boche for tea tomorrow.' All who overheard such remarks and read the story were forced to concede that never had a truer word been spoken. So completely can one man be united with another.

Wherever these people came together, the talk would turn to

Gaston Raille's sensational story; and everyone reminded everyone else over and over again that the name of the hero was Jean Bleuquottoirre. The name was uttered in tones of piety and reverence such as might previously have been reserved for the Lord's Prayer. Its unyielding clangour was sucked in deeply, its brittle conglomeration of consonants was slurped through trembling lips, while eyes rolled as if at the onset of convulsions. Then, once this unaccustomed name had sufficiently performed its work of intoxication, it was let fly with wild abandon, with gasps of rage, with unyielding conviction, with unmistakable and reckless emphasis, and no one neglected to add, 'Why haven't they made this man the Generalissimo? Why not? Because he's just an ordinary man, a man of the people, a worker, that's why. A man without fortune or favour. That's the only reason. Calamity! A thousand calamities! So France will perish because she tramples underfoot the abilities of the man in the street, because she begrudges him the honour of having come to her rescue in her hour of need. She would rather see herself perish first. Calamity! A thousand calamities! The motherland is betrayed! Treachery! Treason!'

Gaston was approached and asked to reveal which regiment the hero served in, so that he might be smothered in comforts and the President be petitioned to enroll him in the Legion of Honour. But Gaston remained silent. And when they kept pestering him, he declared that he had given the man his word not to reveal anything about him, for he was a modest and simple fellow who had done no more than his duty and did not want such a trifle blown out of all proportion.

That this heroic son of the nation could describe such a feat as a trifle! What a man he must be! And what great things might they not expect in the future from one who could call that a trifle!

Now in the charming little town of Montesgaiou in Gascony there lived a mayor. While perusing the *Revue* one day, he came across the story by Gaston Raille. Like all who had read it before him, he found that it made his head spin, but when he encountered the name Jean Bleuquottoirre, a thought flashed instantly through his mind. He was old enough and experienced enough to know that this unusual name, with its remarkably unorthodox spelling, could only occur once in the whole of France, if it existed at all, and the sole possessor of this rare name lived in his municipality and was the shoemaker Pierre Bleuquottoirre.

With the greatest haste, as was certainly indicated here, he ran to the shop where the said citizen eked out his scanty living.

'It's true that you have a son in the army?' he asked, before he was properly through the door.

'Three, Mayor. Dear God, don't tell me that something's happened to one of them.' The old man had risen from his stool and was wiping his hands on his apron, quite by habit, for his eyes were bright with fear.

The major ignored his question and said without further ado, 'One of your lads is called Jean, right?'

'Yes, that's right, yes. Oh, God, so it's the eldest. He was such a good lad, such a smart lad. Oh, this wretched war, this wretched bloody war!'

'He's in the infantry?'

'Yes, in the 467th Regiment.'

'Stationed where?'

'Outside Arras, his last postcard said.'

'You say he's a clever lad, an intelligent sort?'

'Very clever.' (Which father would not believe his son to be the cleverest of all sons?)

'And a machinist?'

'Yes, in Marseilles, before he was called up.'

'Right, right, right! Right in every detail!' The mayor sprang about as though he had taken leave of his senses and shouted, 'Our Montesgaiou is going to be famous, and I'll be famous too. They'll make me an officer of the Legion of Honour, there's no other town can raise heroes like ours.' Then he shook the alarmed Pierre by the hand and said to him earnestly, 'Citizen, citizen, you just don't know... No, it's much more than you deserve. I just don't understand it at all.'

And without offering any explantion to the cobbler, he slammed the door behind him and took to his heels. By the shortest route he sprinted to the offices where Montesgaiou's modest newspaper was put together.

'Now, sir, don't you read the *Revue*? Or are you content to waste your time on all that other trash?'

'Certainly I read the *Revue*,' said the greatly bewildered editor. 'Everyone reads it, you just can't get along without it.'

'Then haven't you read about the phenomenal heroism of our fellow citizen Jean Bleuquottoirre, the son of Bleuquottoirre the shoemaker who lives in the Rue de la Croix? This hero who's serving with the 467th Regiment, presently stationed outside Arras?'

'No, I haven't seen it. With so many newspapers to read, I'm quite happy to let the odd item slip by now and again.'

'Be my guest, then. I've a copy of the *Revue* here in my pocket.'

'But this is a story, not an official communique.'

'What difference does that make? And in any case it's by the famous writer Gaston Raille, and he's been up at the front himself. You wouldn't be thinking he's telling lies by any chance? Why, not even the government would allow communiques to be published if they weren't true. No, you must put this in your paper without fail. Particularly since it concerns a citizen of our town, a child of Montesgaiou.'

And the editor allowed himself to be persuaded that it was his duty to reprint the story and to place the following announcement at its head:

'The hero of this tale, Infantryman Jean Bleuquottoirre of the —th Regiment, which had the privilege of acquitting itself with honour outside Arras, is a child of Montesgaiou and the son of shoemaker Pierre Bleuquottoirre of the Rue de la Croix, who also has two other sons in the army. To the young hero who has brought such great honour to our town we take this opportunity to say, "Bravo, young hero!" The editor.'

The mayor himself saw to it that copies of the Montesgaiou paper made their way to the appropriate destinations in sufficient numbers. And the editor of the paper, who was also its publisher and had no objection to seeing himself and his paper become the focus of attention, had an equally understandable keen interest in promoting an adequate circulation. In view of these and other circumstances, it was therefore no wonder that Generalissimo Joffre eventually summoned the officer commanding the division to which the 467th Regiment belonged, and demanded from him a full account of the heroism of Infantryman Jean Bleuquottoirre. Moreover he expressed his great surprise, his very great surprise indeed, that the commanding officer still seemed rather vague about the precise details and had not yet taken the opportunity to recommend the said infantryman for decoration and promotion; such feats, particularly when performed by common soldiers from modest backgrounds, had to be treated in an especially appreciative manner, otherwise it might appear that only the actions of senior officers were of any importance, and what was more, there was also the business of providing good examples for others to emulate and that kind of thing.

The divisional commander was at something of a loss and excused himself by pointing out that during the recent offensive so brilliantly conducted by the Generalissimo (here he permitted himself a slight but unmistakable bow), so many soldiers had given an outstandingly distinguished account of themselves that it had been totally impossible to establish names and individual performances in the time available; moreover, many soldiers were deterred from pressing themselves forward in the hope of commendation both by their modesty and by their awareness of having done no more than their duty. At all events, he would take immediate steps to ensure that a full report was prepared and submitted within the next twenty-four hours.

The officer commanding the brigade found his temper considerably changed for the worse by a downright peevish instruction from the divisional commander that he should prepare a report; for his commanding officer had spoken of 'an entirely irresponsible negligence which would not be forgotten, should there ever be reason to remember it'. The consequence was that the colonel of the 467th Regiment found himself called to account by the brigadier, and in such a genial manner that the colonel swore he would have resigned his commission had there not been a war on, that being the only possible response to such a slight on his honour as an officer and a gentleman. Nonetheless, he demonstrated his competence as an officer by choosing not to send his call for a report down the extended ladder of descending seniority. Instead, he ordered Infantryman Jean Bleuquottoirre to report to him in person.

At bottom he was proud to have such an able man in his regiment, a man whose prowess had so forcefully brought the 467th to the attention of the Generalissimo, the Minister of War, and the President, that none of them were likely to forget it for some time, or more to the point, until such time as the name of the colonel of the regiment had been ineradicably impressed on their minds. For the common soldier is never more than what his regimental colonel makes of him; the Generalissimo knew that from experience, and those other fellows, by whom he meant the President and the Minister of War, would have to be taught the same lesson in some suitable and effective way.

When the order to send our hero to the colonel was transmitted to the captain who was Jean Bleuquottoirre's immediate superior, it was not long before he realized what was afoot. For the Montesgaiou paper had also found its way to him, and in addition the main outlines of the conversation between the Generalissimo and the divisional commander had been communicated to him posthaste by the divisional adjutant, so that he should not be unprepared in case of need. As for the article in the paper, he had not taken it seriously and with military curtness had dismissed it as 'balderdash'. But now that the colonel had ordered the infantryman to report to him, the captain had no doubt as to what he should do. His lengthy service had taught him quite adequately that to point out the error of his ways to a superior officer is the biggest mistake a subordinate can make. A superior officer is never wrong. Should he be so, then it is proof that his subordinate is unfit to hold a responsible post. Moreover, he is a rhinoceros. And all things considered and carefully weighed, the captain was the soldier's immediate superior, so if this soldier had accomplished some outstanding feat, it could only have been because he had an exceptionally able captain. The Generalissimo, the Minister of War, and the President must surely understand that without having to be told. Indeed, it was all very easy to understand.

Infantryman Jean Bleuquottoirre was ordered to put on a clean uniform and report to the captain. And because Jean was a bit slow on the uptake and inspired little confidence in light of his expression of good-natured stupidity, the captain thought it inadvisable to burden his mind with arduous problems of high diplomacy, which scores its greatest coups by concealing significant facts behind silences and smiles. Besides, bravery and stupidity are closely related as a rule.

And so: 'My lad, you are ordered to report to the colonel.'
'Yes, sir!'
'Is your uniform well brushed? No lumps of muck from the trenches clinging to it? Let's have a look ... that's fine. Now listen here, lad, you're not to be nervous in front of the colonel, you hear. No shaking in your boots as though he were about to bite your head off. The colonel wants only what's best for you, understand?'
'Yes, sir!'
'It's possible that he might also take you to see several generals.'
'Yes, sir!'
'But keep your chin up, you hear? You're from Gascony, aren't you? Then that's something to be proud of. All those gentlemen will want only what's best for you, the very best. They might even give you a medal for bravery. You've earned it, lad, you've always been a good soldier and not shirked drills or run away when the Boche came. So there's no need for you to be afraid, you hear?'
'Yes, sir!'
'And if anyone asks you anything, then all you say is "Yes, sir!", never anything else, understand? It'll make the gentlemen very angry if you contradict them. Just agree with everything they say and answer "Yes, sir!", never more than that, whatever they say. You don't need to bother your head about anything else. Is that clear?"
'Yes, sir!'
'It'll probably be the colonel who asks most of the questions, and he'll want you to tell him all sorts of things you know nothing about, things you've never even heard of. So if at any time you find that the colonel has lost you completely, what you do is to give him this newspaper I'm putting in your pocket and just say, "Here you are, sir, it's all in here in black and white, I've forgotten what happened." Have you got all that?'
'Yes, sir!'
'Fine, then give a good account of yourself, and if anyone asks who your captain is, you say my name loud and clear, right?' He shook the soldier by the hand, then, not wanting to give him time to think things over, commanded, 'And now report to the colonel at the double, left right, left right.' After the first few minutes the colonel knew his man, but he betrayed no sign of emotion, simply

took the newspaper when it was offered to him, clapped the infantryman on the shoulder, and said, 'You're a fine fellow, indeed.'

After telephoning through the usual channels to make arrangements, he and the brigadier drove over to divisional headquarters, where the Generalissimo had just arrived to make an inspection.

Jean was presented to the Generalissimo, who shook him by the hand and said, 'Well done, lad, well done, very well done. From today you are promoted to the rank of sergeant, and I hope that you will continue to be a credit to your famous regiment.' Then, turning to one of the officers who stood beside him, he unpinned his 'Medaille militaire' and affixed it to Jean's greatcoat. 'See to it that this man is mentioned in dispatches tomorrow,' he said, shook Jean by the hand once more, and allowed him to retire.

Then he shook hands with the colonel and said, 'Colonel, I congratulate you, you must be proud to command a regiment that can count such a man amongst its numbers. I hope that you will be doing good work for me in a more responsible position before very long.'

The colonel was about the withdraw when the Generalissimo addressed him once more: 'Oh, by the way, Colonel, I meant to ask you what happened to the two German generals and the colonel who were mentioned in the report as having been taken prisoner? There's something else that I still haven't been properly informed abut. I would have noticed it sooner or later, you know!'

The brigadier turned pale, but the colonel kept his composure and did not flinch under the Generalissimo's stare, either because he had prepared himself to meet this question, or because he really had great presence of mind. At all events he said in his most matter-of-fact tone of voice, 'The three senior German officers, sir, managed to commit suicide with their service revolvers immediately after they were captured, because they could not get over the fact that they had been taken prisoner by a solitary soldier, and a private at that. We didn't want to mention it in our report because in so doing we would have paid the German officers a tribute which might have incurred the displeasure of the population at large; for unfortunately no French officer has yet had the courage to evade captivity in this way. And since the three German officers were indisputably dead, we could hardly include them in our list of prisoners, since someone on the German side would be bound to start asking questions about them sooner or later.'

Maybe the Generalissimo himself was beginning to find the affair rather puzzling. But there was no longer any line of retreat open to him, unless he wanted to make himself look utterly ridiculous.

That he was beginning to have his doubts, however, emerged when he interrupted brusquely, 'Thank you, Colonel!' With a handshake the colonel too was dismissed.

The colonel could have had only the remotest notion of how the whole affair had come about. He could certainly have discovered the truth had he cared to ask a few questions of Jean's captain. But he thought it wiser not to mention the subject again. In the event it was a wish to be shared by both of them, colonel and captain alike, when a few days later the two of them were appointed officers of the Legion of Honour and transferred to more senior posts. Possibly the Generalissimo, thinking of himself, hoped that in this way he would be able to dispel any doubts which might have crept into the minds of the various persons involved.

A similar train of thought prompted the captain to grant Sergeant Jean Bleuquottoirre three weeks' home leave, so that for the time being he would be separated from his comrades. They had become quite curious about his sudden promotion and decoration, but were unable to get to the bottom of it because Jean pretended innocence and claimed to know nothing. And in any case it was just possible that someone in an isolated outpost might have done something which the others had no way of finding out about, for it was only rarely that the company was drawn together in close order. A lot of things might have happened in the foxholes of the forward observation posts.

It was not until he arrived home that Jean learnt of his heroic deed. And for all his outward stupidity, he would have needed to have been entirely lacking in the artful shiftiness of the Gascon not to have realized that he would do better to deny nothing and agree with everything, for why should he want to spoil others' pleasure and deprive himself of all the benefits which accrue to a hero? More than that, wasn't it heroism enough that he had fought in the trenches for eighteen months and taken part in three bloody offensives?

So it was not long before he was squaring his shoulders. He became very proud of himself and his unparalleled bravery and could sit for hours on end recounting the details of his magnificent feat.

It came very easily to him, since he was from Gascony. But do not delude yourselves into thinking that such things can happen only to those who come from Gascony. Paris is closer than you might sometimes imagine.

Mother Beleke

Mother Beleke overcame the tenacious resistance of the Russians and stormed a strongly fortified village. Not that she was present in person. But it was due entirely to her that it was captured with such tempestuous elan by ageing reservists. Those who are acquainted with Mother Beleke will have their doubts, of course, since she is almost seventy years of age and leaves her hamlet only when she has butter, eggs, and fresh vegetables to take to market. But so many seemingly incredible feats of herosim are happening nowadays that nowhere is there anyone who would still venture to remark, 'Oh, that can't be true, it's just not possible!' Not even the most fanciful of souls has it within him to contrive some minor act of valour that has not already been performed in the course of this war by some soldier or some company of troops.

Now although Mother Beleke did not attend in person, this should not be allowed to detract from her triumph. Personal attendance alone is not always what matters most. Even the great commanders are only rarely, or perhaps never, to be found where the battle rages wildest, because that, in the present day, is no longer so easily arranged with any convenience. Nonetheless, it is they who reap the honour of a battle fought and won under their leadership. So why not good old Mother Beleke? True, she herself knows nothing of her glorious victory, but that, too, is neither here nor there. Much more important is the fact of the victory. And it was far from being chiid's play.

Now Mother Beleke had a lad by the name of Herbert. Admittedly, this 'lad' is already well past the age of forty and is moreover a seasoned member of the territorial reserve. One day, before he was given even a moment to think, he found himself called to arms. And was then dispatched at once to garrison a far-distant forward communications zone which lay close behind the front line. Here he remained for two months, 'in exceedingly good spirits', as he invariably wrote in letters to his wife, until he was granted ten days' leave. (Such a feeling of strength and sense of victory there must be in an army which, though engaged in the fiercest of wars, each day sends whole hosts of men on leave, so that they may return home from the front to attend to their private affairs or visit their relations! Can it really be that no one at all has appreciated what that means?)

Herbert's first thought was to visit his aged mother, it being now more than fifteen years since he had last seen her. That need come as no surprise. He lived with his not inconsiderable family in the western part of Germany, while his mother had remained behind in his childhood home in Silesia. And we all know how things turn out in life. The prospect of such a long journey means that the intended visit is always being postponed from one year to the next. First it is the time, then the money that cannot be afforded, then one of the children falls ill and cannot be left, then the wife does not feel up to it, and so it goes on. And before there is time to reflect, ten years have passed and gone.

But now that he was going on leave anyway, seeing that the journey cost so little and he could, as it were, almost reach his native village by stretching his arm out the window of the railway carriage, it seemed only natural to pay a visit to mother at long last. It is easy to imagine that both of them were overjoyed by this reunion, although by now the 'lad' too had a touch of grey in his hair. But a mother never has eyes for such things. Her sons and daughters may grow as tall and as old as they please, in the eyes of their mother they will always remain 'the children'. And a mother

will never believe anything but that her 'children' might fall into
a ditch at some unguarded moment, or eat unripe fruit, unless she
is there to watch over them or at least give them a word of caution
to set them on their way. And so it came about, when Herbert again
took his leave of her two days later, that Mother Beleke kissed her
lad at the station and, knowing no better token of her love and
affection to set him on his way, imparted to him with tears in her
eyes these few well-intentioned words: 'Now, Herbert dear, don't
you be in no hurry to be up and at 'em, them Russkies is a parcel
of rogues.'

The old fellow could not help but be a little moved, though
later, as he sat in the train, he had to laugh; for what Mother imagined
by modern warfare was some kind of brawl not so very different
from a fistfight, except that rifles and sabres were used from time
to time, and here and there a cannon or two.

Naturally, there was much to tell when Reservist Beleke rejoined
his unit. And when to crown it all he reported his mother's parting
words, it seemed that the laughter and hullabaloo would never
come to an end. Nor did it take very long before that winged phrase
became the watchword of the entire company and was being used
at every opportunity, suitable or otherwise.

Then came the day that was to be so memorable for the territorial
battalion. An enforced redeployment of troops had meant that a
section of the line was left unguarded. When the enemy retreated,
a body of soldiers became isolated from the main force. This
isolated unit had discovered the unguarded section and, knowing
nothing of the retreat, had occupied and secured a village which
lay in the breach. It was then that the territorial battalion was
ordered to take possession of the same village. In the headquarters
from which the order came, it was thought that the village was
clear of the enemy and that the communications zone could be
moved forward. And as one company now advanced to carry out
the order, it suddenly found itself matched against an enemy who,
insisting on its own superiority, showed not the slightest inclina-
tion to surrender the village. Thus the advancing unit was caught
in the thick of battle before it had time to take the measure of its
situation. What the old reservists had dreamed of for so long, what
to their immense chagrin had seemed beyond the bounds of possi-

bility, was now a fact. Though a harder one by far than they had imagined.

Now there is more to this business of martial prowess and dare-devil courage than meets the eye. It takes time to adjust to every-thing, even to being fearless and acting courageously. And it is just as well that it should be so. If courage were as much the gift of nature as our appetite for food, then the courage of a soldier would not redound to his glory at all, let alone give him the slightest cause for pride. Just as no one would think to be proud of possessing a pair of lungs; there is simply no choice in the matter. And so it should come as no surprise that at first, when the advance guard was met with machine-gun fire, the old fellows fairly had the breath knocked out of them. Immediately, they threw themselves to the ground as if they had been steamrollered. For quite some time they stirred not an inch and every thought was driven from their heads. Then they took stock of the position and came to the firm conclusion that the village would have to be taken, cost what it might. Headquarters must have had some particular reason for wanting this village to be in their hands. The high command was relying on the order being carried out and had drawn up its plans accordingly. And just suppose that they did not take possession of the village, contrary to orders—who could say what kind of unholy row that might kick up later on? As it was, the entire success of this campaign so far, costly as it had been, could still be thrown to the winds. And neither Hindenburg nor Ludendorff nor Mackensen could put in a personal appearance everywhere to check that things were as they should be. If the order came to occupy the village, it would just have to be occupied, and that was that. It made no difference whether half a regiment of Russians was holed up there or not: if they refused to leave of their own accord, they would simply have to be thrown out. Under no circumstances could the enemy be permitted to obstruct the execution of an order, whatever his strength might be, and by no stretch of the imagination could the enemy be used as an excuse, especially if he happened to be Russian. Well then!

Such were the thoughts of the captain and his platoon com-manders; such too were the thoughts of every reservist. Surely they would not want to find themselves saddled with the reputation of being unreliable? There could be no question of that.

Admittedly, it was much more easily said than done. For the Russians clearly had no thought of running away. They sent a hailstorm of bullets rattling from their machine guns. And as the company now crawled into an attacking position in line extended, the bullets continued to spatter amongst them. There at any rate was something they could heartily enjoy.

Nevertheless, they moved forward. Not that they were in any hurry to do so. But assuredly no one would have reproached them on that account. They were drawing steadily closer. Yet it was the final three hundred metres that proved most hazardous of all. Their rushes became shorter and more and more desultory. Understandably so: the burden of years which weighs on a man's back wherever he goes cannot simply be shrugged off as soon as he hears the word of command. It clings fast. Besides, the Russians could already boast a fair number of hits.

Now there were only about a hundred and fifty paces still to go. To retreat, in fact, would no longer have served any real purpose. Having come so far already, they would surely manage the little distance that remained. And, besides, to withdraw would have cost them more dearly than to advance. Most important of all: the village *had* to be taken.

The captain was considering his next move. From here on he would have to take command of the assault, there was no other way. Indeed, an inexperienced officer would not have hesitated a moment longer before giving the order to charge. But if that order were not carried out, what then? For all the discipline his men had shown so far, the officer thought, that was a distinct possibility, and then he would lose all control over them; they would give way to panic and he would bring back not a single one of them alive. Soldiers are men and not machines, reservists least of all.

Better to wait, thought the captain. There was no respite in the firing from the enemy lines. It only needed the least movement of a shako for a half a dozen enemy machine guns to bark out at once from the other side. But while the captain was still pondering which moment might be best suited to the launching of an assault with some prospect of success, suddenly a cheerful voice cried out, 'Don't be in no hurry, Herbert dear, them Russkies bite!'

The words rang out clearly all along the firing line. They came so unexpectedly that for one brief moment there was total silence. But then it was broken by a laughter so loud and so carefree that the timid began to feel ashamed, while the others sent a stream of jokes dancing into the air above them. And from the midst of all this laughter the same clear voice called out, 'Come on, Herbert dear, up and at the fellows!'

The captain moved to take command. But he was not given the chance. The reservists could bide their time no longer. On the instant a few of them cried, 'Hurrah!', the whole line leapt up and with bayonets at the ready, half laughing still, half roaring, they stormed towards the village. The seriousness of their position by now completely forgotten, they gave not a damn for the Russians or their machine guns. And when they finally came to their senses, it was with the greatest astonishment that they found themselves in possession of the village, having taken eight hundred and seventy Russian prisoners and captured nine machine guns. What they had reckoned quite impossible only a quarter of an hour before, had happened without their really knowing how.

Later, when they came to perform the doleful task of searching for their fallen comrades, they found each one of them lying with a smile on his ashen lips. Can there be a death more enviable than one that is joyful? Why then do you mourn?

Should not all of you, fallen and survivors, be grateful to Mother Beleke? On some she bestowed a triumphant victory, on others a joyful death. And yet it was no more than the solicitude of a loving mother.

In the Fog

Occasionally, when his mind was unoccupied, Sergeant Karl Veek would remember a dream he had dreamt at some time in the past. He could recall the details of his entrancing dream only with difficulty: in it he was a civil engineer who lived a life of sumptuous ease in his own magnificently appointed townhouse, he was married to a wife as attractive as she was sophisticated and had a charming little daughter, and he enjoyed the existence of a diligent, peaceable, and thoroughly contented man.

It was a dream. What made it so entrancing, perhaps, was that it lay at such an unattainable remove. For in reality Karl Veek had been a soldier for as long as he could remember, ever since the age of three at least. He could not recollect that he had ever done anything but wait for the enemy, here in the trench with his rifle at hand. From time to time, in obedience to orders which were exempt from all criticism, he would fix his bayonet and storm the enemy's position, resolutely driving from his mind every thought but this one: every man who stands in my path and wears a uniform different from mine is certain to kill me unless I kill him first, and every noise I hear, be it thunder or gunfire, the rasp of gravel or the rustle of leaves, the sound of a bated breath, in all conceivable probability will mean—my death!

And with his rifle on the parapet in front of him, he fumbled for his pocket. From it he drew a photograph and a letter, thinking it strange indeed that the photograph should bear a distant resemblance to the woman of whom he had once dreamed that she was his wife. And the seemingly so impersonal words contained in the letter, entirely lifeless in themselves, sent an echo ringing through his soul to remind him of the red lips of that beautiful woman in his dream. But so distant was the echo that it might have been the sound of magical silver bells chiming softly below the ground he stood on.

'Sergeant Veek!'

'Here, sir!'

What did dreams ever do for me, thought Veek, but fill my head with foolishness?

'Report to the major at once, Sergeant Veek. Corporal Ehmig will take your post.'

'Very good, sir!'

He was relieved by the corporal and, shouldering his rifle, made his way at the double to report to the major in his dugout.

'Sergeant Veek, I have a tough assignment here, one that needs intelligence. Quite a bit of intelligence. You're the only man for the job, I can't spare any of my officers. So you can see how important I think this business is. There's been no firing from the other side for two days now. No movement of any kind has been observed. Three possibilities present themselves: either the position has been evacuated, or it's a trap, or they're up to something over there. We need to know what's going on. Take two men to give you some support. No rifles, just knives and revolvers. I don't want anyone over there to know that we have a patrol out. Get something to eat and then be on your way. See to it that you're back by nightfall. Any questions?'

'No, sir!'

It was early afternoon, the air was clear. But two hours after Veek set out, a thick, heavy fog settled slowly over the terrain. Then the fog closed in until it was as solid as a whitewashed wall. By now

Veek could no longer make out what lay two paces in front of him. Telling the two men to stay where they were, he went on alone and marked his route back to them by pressing his boot into the soil.

He got to his feet and with short, hesitant steps began to feel his way through the dense white wall, which readily opened one pace in front of him, only to allow him through and then immediately close behind him just as firmly as it seemed to be cemented in front. Fearful that he might lose his bearings, he took out his compass and held it against the small sketch-map.

It was when he raised his head again that he saw, not quite two paces from him, a French officer, who caught his glance and froze in his tracks. Neither of them felt any fear, nor was there fear in their eyes, only a deep stupefaction. Each looked at the other as if he alone had been the only inhabitant of the planet until now, when he suddenly found himself face to face with the first man. At the same moment, as they saw each other's uniform, both thought that now they must do something quite specific, something quite habitual, something commonplace, something which ruled them as if with the force of a compulsion they could not escape, which denied them escape. But neither of them knew what this was, what this compulsion demanded of them. It seemed that there was a voice within them crying out: Act! You know what you must do! But not for years since had either of them encountered, so close and so calm, so unexpected and so alone on this deserted island, a man dressed differently from himself.

Each could sense the other's breathing, each could see even the most delicately inscribed lines in the other's face.

And they stood in great amazement then and suddenly could understand the ways of the world no longer.

At the same moment each of them slowly lifted his hand to his cap and gave a slight but deliberately unmistakable bow in the direction of the other.

Their expressions were severe as death. But in the fathomless depths of their eyes there rested a brief question which men never fail to understand. They lowered their hands. And turned to go.

For the briefest instant there leapt upon them then a second of eternity that stripped them of their uniforms, and unthinkingly, obedient to the one greater will, they reached out simultaneously to take the other's hand, they shook hands in the manner of friends who must part for eternity, they released the other's hand just as quickly, and returned by the way that they had come.

What else was either of them to have done, once he had recognized that standing before him was a man?

For they were both stricken by blindness and did not see the enemy.

The Unknown Soldier

To E.L. 14, a casualty station which lay so close behind the front lines that the dull thunder of the guns could be heard unremittingly were brought only the most severely wounded, those who would not have survived the journey to the rear. By its very nature the work here imposed a tremendous burden on doctors and nurses. And none but the finest of doctors, orderlies, and nurses were appointed to the staff, for only the finest of staff could be of service here.

While the wounded soldiers saw the doctors as indispensable and entirely benevolent presences, it was to the nurses they turned for affection and companionship. Often the soldiers had scarcely set eyes on a woman for months on end, and if by accident they really chanced upon one quite unexpectedly, it would be some wizened crone, always unbelievably filthy and ragged, who bore about as much resemblance to the soldiers' notion of what a female person should look like as a wood louse does to a splendid butterfly. The longer the soldiers remained in the field and the further they were from their homes and accustomed surroundings, all the more did their wives, sisters, brides, and sweethearts appear to them as radiant visions, tender as the palest of roses. And if they then were wounded and brought to the casualty station, where they found themselves surrounded by those ever-smiling women clothed in white who inhabited their dreams, they became like children. The initial shy reserve which they displayed towards the nurses when first they awoke from unconsciousness was little by little transformed into an intimacy of such infinite compassion that it could scarcely be matched by any other human relationship.

The soldier who was admitted to E.L. 14 one evening was discovered by the doctor on duty to have been wounded twice in the lungs and once in the stomach. What could only have been a burst of shrapnel had shattered his thighbone.

His condition was extremely grave. And the man did not recover consciousness. When soldiers have been lying out in the trenches for weeks on end, there is no longer any way of telling them apart. Their faces, their hands, their clothes make them all appear identical. All equally brutalized. And even their speech is for the most part wholly indistinguishable. Rough, abrupt, broken, it has lost those subtle distinctions by means of which the educated man sets himself apart from the less educated. Only days later, once they have bathed several times, have washed and shaved and been provided with fresh linen, do there slowly emerge those social differences from the civilian past which have been acquired in the course of years, not to say generations.

Nothing at all was known about the man who had just been admitted. There was no clue to suggest any possible line of enquiry. The agony of his wounds had caused him to tear feverishly at his clothes and in so doing he had lost his identification tags. Any weapons whose numbers might have afforded some clue had been left behind by the stretcher-bearers, and there was no name sewn into his garments, perhaps because they had been exchanged.

Thus he lay for days on end. His eyes remained closed. Only the sound of his heartbeat and the deep groans he gave at long intervals showed that he was still alive. His thigh had been put into splints. And for the time being the wounds to his lungs and stomach were left to heal by themselves. There could be no question of moving him, if only because of the stomach wound.

The senior physician left instructions that he was not to receive medicines of any kind, either to dull the pain or to rouse him to consciousness, apart from the intravenous feeding which was carried out in the prescribed manner.

The ward in which he had been placed was looked after by Sister Malve. She was the most beautiful of the girls in E.L. 14, and her simple uniform, far from obscuring her charms, enhanced them all the more. She was young, the daughter of a distinguished family, and had been educated in private schools in England and France. Her father was serving as a staff officer on one of the two major fronts. Without a doubt she was the most efficient, the most attentive, and the most tireless of all the nurses working here.

And she it was who was standing by the bed of the unknown soldier, gently stroking his brow, on the very morning when he awoke. He looked at her in amazement, through large eyes which seemed to shine with the light of some long-forgotten world. Then he closed his eyes again and opened them once more, with unutterable incredulity.

After a while he leaned his head gently backwards, so that the hand which rested on his brow came to glide lightly over his face in a tender caress. Then Sister Malve sensed what it was he desired and stroked his face and hands as though he were a child.

She turned from him, intending to bring him something to drink. But he misunderstood. His eyes filled with piteous fear. Sister Malve paused. He reached out hesitantly to take her hand and held it tightly as he said in a low voice, 'Are you a nurse?'

'Yes,' she said.

'Your name is Malve, Sister Malve!'

'How did you know that?'

'I have heard it always, for many years, for so very many years. In a land far away, so very far away from here, I shall return to it, a voice calls out to me from there. Have you not heard it?'

'No, I heard nothing.'

'But it was your name I heard. Malve! Malve!' His voice became slowly fainter. 'Malve is such a beautiful name. As gentle and lovely and lilting and joyful as you are, Malve.'

It was then that she wondered if he had not heard her name spoken by one of the doctors or by his comrades as he lay unconscious.

She was stroking his face again, undecided whether she should call the doctor or rather wait until her patient had fallen to rest once more.

'You are beautiful, Malve. So very beautiful. Never before have I seen a woman as beautiful as you are.'

'Don't you have a wife? What about your parents? Or perhaps there's a girl you're in love with, someone to whom I could send a few words from you?'

'Malve, don't be unkind to me, I have to tell you how beautiful you are. I love you because you have a name that is so lilting and joyful, and even more because you are so beautiful.'

'Try not to excite yourself so, it will only make you feverish. Don't talk so much now.'

'If it pleases you, Sister Malve.'

He placed his cheek against her hand and cradled his face in it Then he began to speak again, more softly now, almost whispering. 'I shall never have a wife, Malve.'

'You shall, you shall, we will make you quite well again.'

'No, I know it. I should like to have a bride. Sister Malve, be my bride. I love you, don't you know that?'

'Yes, I believe you.'

'Be my bride, Malve. For always. Soon I shall be dead and will never have a wife. Say it quickly, say yes, before I am called far away. Will you be my bride?'

Malve blushed and said gently as she bent towards him, 'Yes, my poor friend!'

'Are you fond of me, Malve?'

Tears came to Sister Malve's eyes. 'Yes, I am fond of you, my poor, dear friend.'

And with his large eyes opened wide, eyes which shone with light from that forgotten world, he whispered full of plaintive fear and trembling hope, 'Malve, my darling Malve, kiss me.'

She pressed her lips to his burning mouth. He lifted his arms and flung them about her neck, his lips brushed her ear as he said, 'My darling wife, Malve.'

Then she felt his arms grow slack. Softly she released herself. But he was already dead.

At that moment the senior physician came to the bed with one of the other doctors in order to carry out the usual morning round. He looked at the soldier, raised his eyelids, and said to his assistant, 'Pity, I was thinking only yesterday that I'd manage to pull him through. And no one knows who he is or what he is, where he comes from or what regiment he belonged to, whether he was a private soldier or an officer, a worker or an intellectual or an artist. Just another who'll be posted missing, and maybe someone somewhere will be waiting half a century for him to come home again.' Then he moved on to the next bed.

Sister Malve stood leaning against the wall and wept.

To the Honourable Miss S....

The young lady received the following letter:

Dear Miss S....,

It has fallen to me to perform the scarcely enviable duty of having to inform you that _____ _____ was killed in action on Sunday morning at five o'clock, during an assault on the enemy's position. The fatal bullet pierced his heart. It may be that you will find some small consolation in the knowledge that this assault brought us an unexpectedly great success and was turned into a decisive victory as a result of its exceedingly unfavourable consequences for the enemy. This, no doubt, will weigh lightly with you, given the sorrow you must be feeling, and for the present there will be but one thought in your mind: What use is that to me, if he is dead! Try as I might, I could not bring myself to interpret such thoughts on your part as indicating any lack of patriotism.

I do not know what relationship you enjoyed with the departed, for not once did he mention your name. I am equally in the dark as to the whereabouts of his parents or other relatives. As in all matters which were of a purely personal concern to him, here, too, he remained conspicuously silent. And it was this same profound reticence which prevented any of us from forming a friendship of any intimacy with him. Only on the evening following his death, as I sat speaking of him with several of my comrades, did we make the singular discovery that not one of us could remember having seen him laugh. Such things go unremarked in daily intercourse, all the more so in the field, but while he was alive, it escaped our attention that not once did he ever laugh, or even smile. All of us, myself included, presume that the cause was an excess of longing for someone he had left behind at home. And because there was nothing in his pockets other than this small sealed package addressed to you, it being the only one of his possessions to have any significance, I assume that you were the object of his desires. Although it is generally not the custom for letters to be sent home from the front without prior examination, nonetheless I believe that I may safely take it upon my conscience to forward the enclosed package to you with the seal intact, since in this case it seems to be a matter of a legacy made by the departed. Also enclosed are the medal and bar which we took from his uniform to present to you as a memento.

There is one further point I must add, and I do so directly, in place of the conventional expressions of heartfelt sympathy. All the while I have been on active service—and that is since the day that the mobilization was first declared—I cannot remember that I have ever encountered or heard tell of a soldier who acted with such heroism as the deceased, whose furious desperation would have defied all description even by the most powerful of imaginations. Until the hour of his death he was regarded in the battalion as bulletproof, but I suppose it was simply that his number came up at last.

Permit me to assure you that he will remain indelibly fixed in the memory both of myself and of his and my comrades, and that his name will be bound inextricably to that of the Regiment for as long as the German army remains in existence. We share your sorrow for a hero whose like is seldom to be found, even in an army made of heroes.

> I remain your obedient servant,
>   Nikolaus B.,
>   Captain and Company Commander.

For some time the young lady gazed pensively into space. Only gradually, it seemed, did she arrive at a full realization of what it meant that she should be reminded of him in this manner.

Then she broke the seal.

She found a slim, leather-bound volume, its pages densely filled from first to last with closely spaced handwriting. At the foot of the final page was written:

'There is nothing more for me to say. The consummation has been reached. In my life and in myself. All my thoughts go out to her. Tomorrow death will come. It can take nothing from me, since there is nothing more to take and all its questing is in vain. Now at last it is I who stand triumphant.'

The young lady turned the pages until she came to the first:

Well, what's this? Can it really be mobilization? And war has been declared? By all that exists, is it conceivable that alongside the one and only certain path there runs yet another? This path? This miraculous path, the thought of which lay so far beyond the realms of all possibility?

Out there they are marching through the streets with jubilant clamour. All the little people with their even smaller and more impoverished experience of life are outgrowing their own stature and discovering a goal that is greater than life itself, a goal which will ensure them a place in history; they who otherwise would all without exception have been swallowed up and lost to human memory like grains of fly ash in the ocean.

And I? There is but one thought that concerns me. What care I for life and fatherland? What is war to me? What is this plangent arousal of an entire nation to one mighty purpose of the will? For I stand alone, alone in all the world! As alone and unaided as only a man can be, when suddenly he wakes up to discover as if in a moment of illumination that no one on this earth, not one other single human being, not even the mother who gave him birth, is kindred to him in the ultimate stage of being, that all love and loyalty are nothing but the most unalloyed egoism.

It may be that I committed an unpardonable blunder in preferring discretion to a declaration of my own great love for her. Certainly I cannot demand that she ought to have sensed it. But when for month after month neither she nor I entertained the least thought that did not belong to the both of us, there could be no other admissable conclusion. So, all those to whom I might tell it would say, yours is no more than a pedestrian and tedious love story. And they would find my story, and me not a whit the less, entirely laughable. Just that. And I would concede that they are utterly right to do so. What more could a man do to prove conclusively that he is ridiculous and his story indistinguishable from a thousand others? All of that I freely admit, and a great deal more besides, whatever is desired and demanded of me. Nevertheless, there is none but I who knows that she, and she alone, means life or death to me.

For the rest of my life I might have remained in that frame of mind which has been mine in these past months. There need not have been the slightest change in our relationship, and still I would have felt myself inexpressibly happy, void of desire and wanting for nothing.

Impregnable!

That one idea blinds me to all others. Wherever eyes glance, wherever thoughts carry: the word is everywhere aflame. It can be seen inscribed on the grimy white cement of the pillboxes, visible only from the captive balloon; it floats in the river which meanders around the fort; it hangs from the lush grass on ramparts which have never felt the scythe; it lingers in the glances of the populace, be they indifferent or ironic; it parades itself through the manuals of military science and architecture, not only the yellowed and decaying tomes, a thousand years old and decipherable only by aged scholars who can hardly tell a cannon from a rifle, but also the volumes bright as a new pin, written by men of whom it cannot be determined whether they are exceptionally gifted scholars or equally gifted soldiers.

But the officers of the besieging army give a raucous laugh when they hear the word spoken; the younger ones merry and carefree, the older ones with ponderous calm and conviction.

We were to attack by night, without preliminaries. By surprise. Why did not I act in that way? By stealth, by surprise. And then to die. Death would have been a fitting prize indeed.

'Take five men over to that coppice right away. The artillery in the fort will be pounding those trees throughout the night, but come what may it's your duty to hold the edge of the wood.'

'Very good, sir!'

The night attack did not succeed. And I was glad of it, for it proved to me that a surprise assault was bound to fail and that I have no cause to reproach myself with any neglect; for failure would have been an ignominious crime. And because the garrison of the fort thought it possible that we might use the coppice as a point of support during the imminent attack, every tree and every fibril of moss had been wiped from the face of the earth before dawn. Over the entire sector the ground had been furrowed to a depth of many metres by some giant plough which had passed over it.

My five men were dead. Their blood and fragments of their flesh adhered to my uniform. I was unscathed. And in the morning an advance patrol sent out by the enemy to occupy the coppice as an outpost was forced to retreat with its mission unaccomplished. When my first shot rang out, they halted as if petrified, so astonished were they that anyone could still be alive and capable of defending he position. They tried to run, but not one of them got back.

With a few giant strides my company came storming forward to occupy the sector, which afforded excellent cover now that the ground had been churned up and pitted by innumerable shells.

When the captain caught sight of me, he exclaimed, 'What? You're still alive? I thought—' 'Yes,' I replied, 'still alive, and not without reason.' 'What d'you mean?' he asked, fixing me with his eyes, but he had no time to wait for my answer.

We dug until we were gasping for breath and the steam rose from our clothing. All the while the shells were raining down on us. Afterwards we sat in the safety of our foxholes and called to each other in the cheerful exhaustion of a task completed, 'Well, we managed it after all!'

Only now, it appeared, did the garrison realize that its patrol had been unable to hinder our advance. Convinced that this was a vital strongpoint, those in the fort began to direct a devastating fire onto our position. But we were well dug in ....

The night was close and heavy. Searchlights probed towards us from the other side, winkling us out of our foxholes, all of us, each in his turn, so that we felt as if we were crouching on white sawdust in the middle of a circus ring, entirely enveloped in a blinding glare and under the merciless scrutiny of an immeasurable ocean of cruelly curious eyes. We came to fear that glare and those eyes horribly. We dared not speak, nor even breathe. We had only one idea in our heads, to burrow ever deeper, yet we did not have the courage to make even the slightest movement.

Under that blinding glare I felt again that she was resting her eyes upon me with enervating indifference, while I leant against the window-frame with Inge's tousled boyish head held against my breast. She was too generous a person by far even to know the meaning of jealousy. Though scarcely half an hour before we had been sitting together in the most intimate proximity, such as exists solely between man and wife in those moments when their minds are fully occupied with the intensity of their friendship, when they are held in the sway of the one single idea: Let what is unspoken between us never be said, never come to fulfilment! And nonetheless their common desire is to be flung headlong and trembling into the great transformation: Let the thought be spoken aloud!

And in that hour when one quails before fulfilment, because there is no way of telling whether it will destroy the more beautiful and perfect state of being, then it was that she said, 'Such is my respect for you, such is my confidence and boundless belief in the inherent nobility of your spiritual life, that I would not imagine it possible for you to conceive an infatuation of that commonplace kind which is taken up and cast off according to whim and convenience. You are of that extinct species which can grasp only two ideas: either—or!'

She did not say it to flatter. That was not within her nature. But she presented her judgement, which contained infinitely more between the lines which we two alone could recognize and understand, as an established fact which she had ascertained by means of a searching examination of my personality. As proud as a chemist who finds that the calculations made in his study yield a perfect result when tested in the laboratory, so proud she must have been as she pronounced this final verdict.

What made me feel so exalted and gave me infinite happiness was that for the first time in my life I had found someone who was at pains to read the book of my soul and to understand that part of myself that I was still uncertain of. I acquired a sure belief in my own abilities; quite new and unsuspected forces urged me to make a resolute start on all that I had previously thought impossible, to take up again plans that I had discarded long before and carry them through regardless.

'Yes, you're right,' said the sergeant-major who was lying beside me, 'you're quite right, if we don't carry on regardless and make a resolute start within the next half-hour, we'll be mincemeat.'

The sergeant major, a corporal, and I were positioned some distance ahead of the actual front line. We were manning the field telephone. The sergeant major lay with the set beside him and the earpiece in his hand, while I took notes and the corporal observed the terrain.

The sun rose into the sky. Several shells prodded the ground in front of us, giving off spectacular amounts of smoke. We came to the conclusion that the enemy was trying to range his guns for the offensive that was expected to begin that day. The projectiles bored their way into the soil like plump fingers, with all the calm deliberation of elderly philosophers. Invariably, when they had burrowed deep enough, they exploded with a shattering roar. It looked and sounded as though no harm at all could come of it, as though this probing were some innocuous and elaborate game. But still the sergeant major flinched each time, and the corporal pressed his head into the churned-up earth with every whine he heard. I said to him, 'Why do you always duck your head like that?' He looked at me, but said nothing. His face was quite pale.

The shells came over in an almost perfectly straight line. The thought came to me that the enemy gunners, after every hit and every impact, were carefully entering into a small grey notebook beside them both the elevation and direction of the gun, as well as the time of detonation, as if they were on a firing range. Since they were familiar with every last centimetre of the surrounding terrain to a radius of at least twelve kilometres, all they seemed to be doing now was to be verifying what they already knew.

Then the sergent major said, 'I'm not sure, but I think the line's been damaged since I haven't had any reply for some time now. What should we do?' 'Check the line, what else?' I replied. The sergent major: 'With this shelling going on? And there's infantry in advanced positions a thousand metres in front of us, as I hope you've already noticed for yourself. D'you really think they'd let a target get through?'

'No, of course I don't think that. They wouldn't be much use as soldiers if they did. But I'll go all the same, the walk will do me good!' I said and rose to my feet. I could have crawled. But what would have been the point of that? It would only have delayed the necessity by one day or by two or three.

The spike was torn from my helmet at once, then I felt something tug lightly at my trousers below the knee, just where they were tucked into my boots. I looked to see what it was and found two bullet holes the space of three fingers apart. Then something slammed into the heel of my boot, a shot had buried itself in the leather. But the only thing on my mind was what she had said that day: 'I have been deceiving myself. Do you realize how thoroughly ashamed that makes one feel? That it makes one appear in one's own eyes as the perpetrator of some loathsome crime? Such a humiliation is not something to be forgotten.'

That settled the issue.

So far there had been no break in the line. I looked at the thick grey cord slithering over the ground. Life and death vied closely together inside it, in its thin red nerve fibre, each in turn racing the other. In one place it had been struck by a shell. But it had only been pressed into the soil, and when I pulled it away I found that it was unscathed. It was flexible and tough.

I should have been so, too. Would it have made me any happier now? I think not. Once it has begun to totter, it is futile to try to buttress an edifice which was believed to be unshakable until the end of time. On the next occasion it will only totter one degree more. But I could at least have told her that Inge, who had come running up the stairs in a frenzy of exuberance to share some innocuous piece of gossip with her, had been suddenly overtaken by an indisposition and would have collapsed against the window sill had I not been standing there. And just at that moment she had entered the room. It was as far from her mind as from my own to suspect anything that might have required a different interpretation. Of that I was convinced. And it was precisely because I was so sure of it that I was unable to pretend nonchalance. My thoughts were still circling restlessly around our last conversation. Hers too. And between those words which had afforded me such uncommon happiness and my answer, there stood this innocent woman. Her eyes betrayed no astonishment, no sign that she had been taken unawares, but all the same I said, 'Miss Inge was in such a hurry that she tripped and would have fallen if I had not been standing here.' At once she sensed the insult that I had unintentionally done to her, and in my voice there was a tone of such eager apology that she must have felt the hurt twice as keenly. She grew pale, and I noted how quickly she had to move across to the table in order to support herself at first. But immediately she said, 'Really, my dear, do you feel unwell? Come out with us, we were about to go for a drive. It will make you feel better.'

The cable was undamaged. But the captain, the warrant officer, and the two privates who had been manning the other end of the line were all dead. A shell had burst in their midst. I checked the receiver and found it to be in good working order. I did not trouble to move the bodies out the way, since there would be time for that later and in any case I had to step between them to get to the telephone. Then I had a word with the sergeant major, who sounded glad to hear a human voice. During the time that his set had been out of action, he had had the feeling of being in an abandoned position, a horrible sensation second only to loneliness. However, I did not tell him that the men at this end had all been killed; instead I gave him to understand that there was only one man here and that he had been wounded. Then I set out at a run for battalion headquarters. Before long I met someone else who had also been sent out to enquire into the break in communications, for the telephone which the captain had been using was connected by one line to the company occupying the advanced post and by another to battalion headquarters.

I explained to the soldier what had happened and sent him to the company's position with instructions to set up a new telephone link at once, then pass on the details to battalion. I returned to my post. The corporal had been wounded in the leg and was unable to move. He gave the unmistakable impression of being quite cheerful about this, because now they would have to send him home. But he had to remain with us for the moment, in spite of his pain, since we could not spare him in case anything should happen to us.

I chanced to look up and thought I saw the terrain moving. A patrol was moving up on us, crawling on their bellies. It was composed of only five men. 'If they don't come too close and catch sight of us,' said the sergeant major, 'we'll leave them to do as they like. Then the others will be all the more certain to follow.'

The patrol moved off to one side. Then the shelling started up again, probing just as slowly and cautiously as it had that morning. Half an hour later I took up the receiver to report, 'Sergeant major Schütz has just been killed.' Back came 'Are you alone in the observation-post?' 'Yes,' I answered, 'Corporal Klein was badly wounded in the leg by a shrapnel burst and has died in the meantime. It was while he was trying to bandage him and stop him bleeding to death that the sergeant major was hit.' 'Nothing further to report?' 'No.'

And then came the night. I sat waiting for the two replacements who had been promised me, but they did not arrive. The two bodies lay beside me. I had to keep looking at them, not wanting to, but unable to avoid it. All the time I was thinking that at least one of them would wake up, because it seemed so inexplicable that neither of them would say one word more for the remainder of eternity, that now it was all over as far as they were concerned. What use would victory or defeat be to either of them now? Only the living have feelings, after all. And I am an egoist. Nothing if not a convinced egoist. What do I care about the war? I know what conscious purpose has drawn me here, and I await its fulfilment with impatience. In any case I cannot make myself out to be any better than I am, and certainly have no wish to act out a comedy of make-believe for my own sake. Above all not in these pages which will remain unread until after my death, for I shall not be taken prisoner, not alive. Others are more noble, in their own opinion, and they are right to think so. But they ought to concede that I am right as well.

I lay in an ocean of light. The long white streamers advanced toward me from the other side and approached me from behind. But the two replacements did not come. Perhaps they had been killed on the way, or had lost their bearings. At all events I would not enquire, and since no one asked me either, that relieved me of any need to supply an answer. With luck they would simply neglect to send anyone to join me. In truth, I could do without their company. They bore me, all of them, though sometimes I feel regret that I have no friends amongst them.

There is no denying that I might have searched out a new and different task in life, found a different purpose to life. Yet I simply did not want to. Why should I have? Was I supposed to babble away, perhaps, concocting theses and explanations to point up something that glittered as softly as shimmering sunlight in the air between us? I could see no reason to do so. What has once been ravaged is beyond repair. And whatever the accommodation we might have arrived at by means of explanations and windy propositions about the misunderstandings between us, even though it might perhaps have provided us with an entirely new beginning, all the same it could not have been other than an artificially patched-up affair. And afterwards I could not have failed to notice those patches again and again, and neither could she. It would have meant living in eternal anguish that one day a new patch might be needed somewhere else. Since I had no desire to be thrown this way and that by my fears of an ultimate and mortally wounding loss, since I love myself too well to be a pendulum, so there remained to me only one final pathway. But how to reach its end?

Hence my utter indifference: I rose to my feet, took my rifle under my arm, and walked forward, in the direction of the fort. That was the shortest and surest way. The searchlights were stabbing at the landscape like fists thrown with lightning speed. Then the fists were drawn back again, only to strike elsewhere with the same instant swiftness. Where the fist landed there would immediately appear, like some fabled magical landscape torn from the satiated darkness, the most miraculous image: silvery-white grass, pale blue furrows of earth, ruby-red bushes, their outlines shrill and harsh, their sharpness painful, all invested with the most improbable colours and with eerily insubstantial shadows.

Had I stood in the path of one of these fists, the bullet would have found me. What point was there in seeking it myself? By leaving it to another I would remain innocent. Or perhaps not? So be it, I would earn the bullet honourably. 'Halte là! Qui vive!' came the sudden cry from in front of me. 'Jackass,' I shouted back, and stood motionless. 'Approchez!' called the voice in front. No, I thought to myself, that is one pleasure I shall not give you. I threw myself to the ground. All was silent once more, the heavy darkness left me with the feeling that I was floating in an ocean of nothingness. Reflecting on what the next step should properly be, I told myself that I might as well stay where I was for a while longer. And during that time I made a discovery which would have to be passed on to the company. A whole battalion was dug in here, along a line at least three kilometres in length, and the attack planned for one o'clock that night could not succeed without further preparation. It was no fault of all the thousands of my young comrades that life was a matter of indifference to me.

I waited. But nothing stirred. They were confused. Perhaps they believed that it was one of their own men who had wandered off. They did not open fire, in order not to betray their position. They had not been there the day before, I knew that for a fact. So the searchlights had served the vital purpose of screening them as they moved into position. Behind the fists the darkness was that much thicker and more impenetrable.

By this time I had lost all interest in myself and in my real intention. I realized that only when I suddenly had the rather uncanny feeling that there was a man lying two paces ahead of me. I could sense his breathing, and so I kept my own face close to the ground. Now at last the long-awaited moment which I yearned after for so many weeks had arrived. I needed only to lie low and all would be well. Just then I had no thought at all for my duty as a soldier, or for the fatherland. Like my egoism, it seemed to me, all of that had been snatched away to some eternally unapproachable and nebulous distance. I could not even begin to describe the nature of what was passing through my mind. Drawing my bayonet with infinite slowness and stealth, I thrust myself forward, not crawling, but relying on my muscles and my yearning, and plunged my bayonet into the ponderous mass before me. Something warm flowed over my outstretched hand. I pushed myself another pace forward and wrenched both epaulettes from the ungainly mass. When I had also got hold of his kepi, I crept back, rising to my feet after ten paces to return swiftly to my position, while keeping a careful count of my steps on the way. I was able to find my post only because I stumbled over the corporal.

The white streamers flickered across the black field like weird apparitions. The two corpses lay close behind me. Once I had switched on my torch, I wiped my bayonet on my trousers to remove the red stain. But most of it did not come off, but stuck fast.

Then I spoke to the company post. They had called several times and had already given me up for dead. The two men sent to operate the telephone had still not arrived. I had myself put through to the commanding officer. 'What's that you say?' the lieutenant colonel called agitatedly into the telephone. 'What, you mean the terrain in front of forts eleven and thirteen is occupied by infantry?' 'Yes, sir, infantry and machine-gun sections, as far as I could see, with about one machine gun every hundred metres.' 'There's no chance you're mistaken? We've reconnoitred the ground and none of our patrols came across anything like that.'

It made no difference to me whether or not I managed to convince the colonel that his patrols had blundered. So I said, 'From my present position it is exactly nine hundred paces to the occupied terrain.' To which the colonel replied, 'Soldier, if what you say is true, then it'll be thanks to you if we capture the two forts, and at least four thousand of your comrades will owe you their lives and limbs.'

I looked at my watch. It was twelve o'clock. What must have happened was that the enemy had captured one of our patrols, and the lads in their stupidity had let themselves be tricked by skillful cross-examination into revealing that the surprise attack on the outer forts was scheduled for that same night. It was out of the question that the commandant of the redoubt could have had any inkling that we would take up position and then immediately attempt an assault on the very next night without a massive artillery barrage. He would have been reckoning on four weeks beyond any doubt.

An appalling silence reigned. In the evening, at least, the crickets had chirped and the frogs had croaked by a pond somewhere. But now only the long bars of light swept like wraiths through the darkness, casting their fairy landscapes, like puppets, from one

side to another. At length the silence was such that I conceived a
fear of my own heartbeats and did everything I could think of to
check my breathing. In suffocating tension I listened for some
sound to indicate that one of the corpses was moving and about
to speak. Even now I could not bring myself to believe that they
had been swept from the face of the earth and were a part of it no
longer. When I heard no such sound, I thought they had vanished.
I wanted to look for them by the light of my torch, but it would
be seen from the other side. When I could bear it no longer, I took
my rifle and thrust it towards the place where the two of them lay.
They were lying there still. Both of them. It raised my spirits
somewhat.

Then I heard a clattering noise overhead. It might almost have
been a quail. And shambling in its wake, as if it had been left
behind, there came a thunderous roar which then made off as fast
as it was able, so that it could be heard only far away in the distance.
It was like a deliverance after that terrible silence. I felt alone no
longer; I felt that behind me still there were men who were on my
side. That left me with a sense of elation such as I had never felt
until that hour. Now the air was filled with a roar that threatened
to drive the breath from my body at any moment. But after it had
lasted for some time, I was again overtaken by the same tearing
anguish at being alone and abandoned, just as before during the
silence. So minutely small, so abandoned by God and all the world
did I imagine myself in the midst of that terrible roaring, that I
began to weep like a little child. It was not fear. It would not have
mattered to me if I had been hit. The heavy guns of the redoubt
roared from the other side in answer to the barking of the guns
behind me. And between them I lay so hopelessly alone and forgotten. At that moment I had neither friends nor enemies any
longer and was overwhelmed by an inexpressible sadness. I had
only one desire: that a merciful shell might finish me. For the first
time it was not egoism that filled me with that ardent desire, for
the first time I did not see it as a means of achieving my purpose
that I might become a casualty. And not for a moment did I think
the thought that had been with me since my life with her came to
an end, though just then I could have answered for it joyously
before the court of eternity.

The long white beams of light had been extinguished, both in front of me and to my rear. They were quite superfluous now. As long as this barrage lasted, neither side would mount an attack. The guns were so well concealed that it was not possible to see the flash as they fired. I had become so accustomed to the roaring that it scarcely penetrated my mind, and I was thoroughly persuaded that above the thunder I should not have missed hearing the crack of a dry twig trodden underfoot.

I looked around and caught sight of a solid mass advancing ponderously towards me on a broad front. Black, impenetrable, and threatening, it stood out against the dull gleam of the night sky. Then, as if half-asleep, I heard between the peals of thunder a frenzied gasping and a furious pounding of feet. It reminded me of the frantic pounding and gasping, quite unlike anything else, of a herd of buffalo fleeing from a prairie fire.

I leapt to my feet and shouted, 'Comrades, comrades!' But I was promptly knocked to the ground and trampled on. Our men pounded on over me. One of them fell and became entangled in our covered shelter. Two others fell across him, so that I was now lying beneath them and protected from the third, fourth, and fifth ranks which came after. But it lasted only for a brief moment, then the ones who had fallen over me leapt to their feet and raced after their unit. Not one word did I hear spoken, not one command given, but when they were about three hundred paces away from me, I heard a shrill whistle. And almost at the same moment a boisterous 'Hurrah!' rang out in front of me.

They had overrun the advance positions of the enemy, already gnawed at by the artillery, in the first onslaught. But the onslaught broke against the ramparts of the redoubt and splintered like a forest under the onrush of an avalanche. Their bodies could carry them no further, though the will was already two thousand metres past and beyond. The ramparts were studded with mines, with traps, with machine guns, and with fully rested and amply fed troops who sat in their concrete foxholes in such calm security that for them it was a jolly shooting match.

The first rank drowned in blood. The second thought to avenge their comrades, and in their blind fury stormed almost defenceless onto the bayonets and the sharp steel wire. Like sacks they rolled down from the mighty ramparts, into the arms and between the feet of the third rank's troops. And as a result the third rank lost its momentum and impulsive speed and formed knots and clusters. And these knots and clusters tore the fourth rank into helpless fragments, threw the onrushing fifth and sixth ranks into inextricable confusion, and turned their bodies, fists, weapons, and boot leather against the seventh rank. The whole great mountainous chain of screaming, bleeding, fighting, fleeing, groaning human bodies threw itself in frenzied fear against the following three ranks, which were being brought up with a hearty song to rescue from destruction their comrades who had come to grief and to turn the battle in their favour. But though their song still filled the air in isolated spots, hearty and triumphant and certain of victory, its gruesomely impressive loudness attempting to drown the thunder of the guns, elsewhere the song mingled with the screams of madness from the fleeing soldiers, a mass entangled in itself and seized with mindless horror. The singing burst out and died away like a fire flickering out. Into the place of a jubilant rendition of the final lines there stepped fury, the raging fury of the thwarted. But while they sought an outlet for their frenzy in violence, they were dragged almost effortlessly by a great, chill, and indifferent hand into the wild and unstoppable flight of the heap of humanity which as a mass has become unpredictable. From behind them came shells, shrapnel, and rifle bullets, jostling for precedence. It was horror become human, the great intangible horror. And the horror was illuminated by the long beams of light which flitted back and forth, now on one side and now on the other; a picture torn brutally from the void of blackness, they seized it roughly as if between forceps, then shook it about and finally released it to throw it back again into the night.

I shall not claim that I, for my part, would not have allowed myself to have been swept along so unresistingly in this mindless mass. Only someone who had been in the midst of the heap could say what he would have done. But a mass thought, even when it is madness become real, does not allow any weight to the individual mind, however directly it may be descended from God. Here the individual is no more than the powerless tiny speck in the dust of the street as it is whipped along by the storm, no more than the miserable drop in the ocean spray. But at all events I would have tried not to succumb to frenzy. Even if I had had to do so only in order to set myself against the majority. Later I heard that the men had felt mortally ashamed of their sudden panic, which appeared quite incomprehensible to them on the following day.

I had remained in my foxhole and saw it all quite clearly through my field glasses. At any moment one spot would be picked out in the harsh light and plunged into the deepest darkness immediately afterwards. If this spot was then wrenched glaringly from the void once more, the picture it presented was altered down to the smallest detail each time. But it was always that of a swarming heap of human bodies. And all the time I kept thinking that it was not true, that it was a lurid dream. Then the telephone buzzed, I heard orders and gave reports and knew that I was awake.

It was then that I wanted to join the wild advance; I could bear it no longer. But the order came through: 'You are not to leave your post under any circumstances, even if a withdrawal back to our lines should become necessary; the observation post must remain in operation. The new code word for the beginning of each message is "Rummelsburg", and after the final word of every second sentence the countersign is "Muritz". Report at once if you have the slightest suspicion that the code word has been overheard by anyone listening in. Got that?'

'Yes, sir!'

The masses came flooding blindly back. They blundered over me, trampled the foxhole we had constructed so painstakingly, kicked me bloody and raised bruises on my head with their boots and trailing rifle butts. One man passed by with his haversack dangling loose and half-torn from him. It was crammed full, and I remembered that I had not eaten anything for almost twelve hours. 'Let me have your bread ration!' I shouted to him, and since he did not hear me, seized hold of the haversack in order to tear it away from him. It did not come free at once. The fleeing man thought that I was trying to hold him back. He turned round and screamed like a madman, 'You bastard!' and stabbed at me with his bayonet. He slashed my arm. He did not get his rifle back under control quickly enough and was about to abandon it, but at the same moment some of the discipline that had been drilled into him returned, and he bent to pick it up. I saw his face. It was contorted with hideous fear. In the brief second that he was close to me, I said to him, 'Comrade, what did you stab me for?' He returned to his senses for a moment. With the staring, confused eyes of the fever-stricken he peered at me, and when he saw that he had stabbed a comrade while thinking that he was being held by the enemy, he cried, 'Sorry, sorry, comrade!' With precipitate haste he then snatched up his rifle, gripped his haversack more tightly with his other hand to prevent it from getting between his legs, and raced away across the battlefield, almost made insane by the return of his mortal fear.

The pain which had quivered in his voice left me bitterly distressed. I would have given a lot to have been able to let myself go for a moment and bawl. There was a constriction in my heart, my eyes, and my throat.

Now I understood everything and everyone. When I first saw them rushing about as they had, I thought: Sloppy bunch! But now I thought so no longer.

The deluge of the masses ebbed away. I began to put the foxhole back into some kind of order and to prepare myself for what lay ahead of me. For it was improbable to the highest degree that the garrison of the redoubt would not make a sortie to complicate the reforming of the shattered units.

Some men came past, unable to run as fast as the others because they had been wounded. All those who passed close by, within range of my shouts, fell forfeit to me. When the idea first occurred to me, I intended it entirely for my own amusement, to pass the time. But then, when I observed that in the circumstances the stakes were very high, I set to in earnest. And did not abandon my plan, even though it put me in danger of being punished for overstepping the bounds of my authority.

'Hey there! Where d'you think you're going?' I shouted to the first man who came limping by. He was wearing only one of his boots and his other foot was wrapped in what looked like a blood-soaked rag. 'Back to my company!' 'Nothing doing,' I said, 'you can give up that idea. You stay here with your rifle till I tell you to go.'

'You can keep your mouth shut, understand?'

'If you take one more step and don't come over here this instant, I'll shoot you where you stand!'

He came to attention and answered in a completely mechanical way, 'Yes, sir!'

I set him to enlarging the foxhole. In the meantime I kept my eyes open so that I could get hold of more of this type. Each and every one tried to get out of it. 'I've had orders to return to my company at once,' the next one said. I could readily imagine that no one had found time to issue that or any other order in the wild confusion of the rout. Nevertheless, I made a pretence of believing it and said, 'You know the order that counts is the last one to be given.' At that he became docile and obeyed. The next, who offered a similar excuse, was answered with, 'No one in the company will realize you're missing, you might just as easily have been made prisoner as killed.' One went limping on his way and paid no attention to my shouts. When I called after him that I would shoot him instantly if he did not return at once, he showed not the least sign of obeying. Good as my word, I fired at him and hit him in the leg. That knocked him hollow, and he came crawling laboriously towards me, since he was wounded in both legs, and asked to be forgiven. 'You can thank your lucky stars if I don't put you on a charge for refusing to carry out an order given in the field.'

None of them grumbled. They peered at me, obviously at a loss to know what to make of me, and since I was no longer speaking familiarly to them, they believed that they were dealing with an officer disguised in a private's uniform for the purpose of some soldierly ruse or other. They did everything I instructed them to. And because they were aware of being under orders once more, they rediscovered the best part of their previous military bearing. First I saw to it that each of them was bandaged, as well as was possible, and then the shovels flew like crazy.

'You muttonheads, aren't you all ashamed of running away like a pack of old women? Which stinking parade ground did they teach you that on?'

'Well, all the others were running away and so we ran too.'

'Like a flock of sheep!'

'We just got carried along.'

'Did you now? And everyone will have the same story to tell.

You're men to be hellishly proud of, that's for sure.'

'I don't know how it happened either. I'm no panicmonger, truly I'm not. But once it had started, the running away, then at first it was quite impossible to know what was going on. Everything got mixed up, and there was nothing for it but to run with the rest, since after all you can't take on a whole redoubt on your own.'

What they said was no less than the truth. That was just how it would have been. If the fire alarm is sounded in the theatre, even though no one sees the smallest lick of flame, the same thing happens. Why should it be appreciably different in battle, when everyone's nerves are stretched by that much more, and in the midst of a thunder and uproar that cannot be surpassed. The people are just the same.

'We feel ashamed,' two of them said.

'Well, now you have an opportunity to make up for it, which is something the others who're with the battalion at the rear cannot do. They shall not pass this spot we're standing on. The position is to be held.'

'Yes, sir, it's to be held.'

I did not correct their notion that I was an officer, for it occurred to me at the time that I might be able to make use of it. The eventuality that they might show themselves recalcitrant could not be ruled out, and since they outnumbered me—and since I, of course, could not prove to them the extent of my authority to issue orders—they might simply have run away.

In the meantime our number increased to seventeen. Some of them managed to evade me after I had called to them, because I was unable to keep them in sight during the perpetual gaps between the white streamers of light. But those who had stopped here would remain here. I felt marvellously certain that I could rely absolutely on every one of them. Out of chagrin at their weakness they assumed a kind of doggedness, to prove that they were also capable of acting differently. By now they were already helping to get hold of still more men. Swiftly I organized them into sections and appointed section leaders. The trench was being extended in length by the minute.

Several times enquiries came down the telephone about whether any of our troops were still in no man's land. They wanted to start the barrage and keep no man's land under protective fire, because there were fears of a counterattack. And then there was some trouble with the reserves.

The crash of heavy gunfire from the other side had not ceased for a moment. It was only when our imminent bombardment was mentioned over the telephone that I began to notice it again. During the whole of this time I had been completely deaf to the continuous thunder of the artillery.

Searchlights traversed the battlefield from both sides—ours to guide the returning men and theirs to make better targets of the fleeing. Whole sections were mowed down. But we were relatively safe.

I felt quietly annoyed that no one had asked me over the telephone whether I was still bearing up or whether I would like to be relieved or whether I still had any food. But then I thought that I really had no reason to be properly angry about it, for those at the rear would surely have more important things to think about just now and would themselves probably not manage either to sleep or to eat, and it went without saying that we had to remain at our posts. But despite that they might still have asked at least, since I am not a dumb animal.

No, in truth, I am not a dumb animal and am just as fully entitled to my life as any other, and not only to life itself, but also to some happiness in life. Really, I need not have taken it so very tragically at the time; I might even have reconciled myself to it, as everyone else manages to do. Without mutual toleration there is no chance at all that people will be able to live alongside one another. I ought to have remained quietly at my post. But nonetheless I felt that the position was a hopeless one. It is the most serious error people can commit that they try over and over again to paste together something that is absolutely bound to fall apart under all circumstances. They should let things fall apart, and even hasten the process, but not paste over them. And when things become unbearable, then they should walk away and leave it all behind. But I am not robust enough to forget and look for substitutes. So there is only one thing left for me to do. And that decision remains firm, irrevocably so.

Let them come at us. I would not retreat one foot of the way. Where was there to go? Since the end result would still have been the same for me, why should I not combine my over-all intention with the business of adding a few complications to the situation. It would make something of a change, after all, and not many people have ever had such a fine opportunity to combine the necessary with the heroic.

I was startled from my thoughts by the fact that the gunfire from the other side was ponderously contemplating whether it might get some sleep. Everything gets tired sooner or later. To me it was a sure sign that something was about to happen. And when a finger of light rested for a while longer than intended on one spot in the terrain, I observed through my glasses that they had completed their regroupment and that the troops detailed for the counterattack were being brought gingerly forward. They would have to hurry if they wanted the mantle of night to cover them, for it would be daylight in an hour.

There were twenty-nine of us now. Because the trench was taking up too much of our time, I told them just to dig foxholes as deep as a man, but to spread them over a wide area. The men understood what I was after much better than I could have explained it to them.

Those people over there ought to have chosen a different route by which to make their counterattack, then they would have come out of it better. But they followed precisely the same route that our masses had taken as they flooded back. Their assumption was correct. That route would without doubt have led them to our Achilles heel.

None of them had thought to find such an obstruction lying in their path, and so close to their front line. They had trained their powerful lights on the battlefield behind the fleeing men, yet had seen nothing other than the disorderly retreat.

They came with their heads held high and their rifles held loosely in their hands, totally sure of their eventual success, and such was their unconcern that they took almost no precautions. Their searchlights were directed onto our front lines far ahead of them, leaving them in deepest shadow, while our lights were scurrying and flickering no more than timidly across the terrain. The counterattack was not thought to be so hard on our heels.

Half bent to the ground, I ran the length of the three hundred metres or more which we now occupied and ordered the flanking sections to direct their guns far out to the left and right, in such a way as to feign the appearance of an occupied front line at least twice as long. The comrades were feverishly excited at finding themselves with an opportunity to act like soldiers again. 'We won't desert our posts, you can rely on that,' they told me. And I replied, 'That goes without saying.'

The enemy were about four hundred metres from us. At that point I ought to have telephoned to the rear and reported that the devil was afoot here. But I could not do it; I was negligent of my duty, knew it and felt ashamed because of it, yet still did not do it. In any case I did not give a copper penny for myself as an individual, whom I had completely renounced. So why stop now?

From the other side a barrage was being laid down far to the rear of my line. It must have been landing immediately in front of our main line of trenches and was intended to prevent us from finding the peace and quiet to assemble and regroup our forces. But our gunners had had their forty winks and opened up again. Too late, of course. Had they been as diligent half an hour earlier, then admittedly they would have hit many of our own men. That would have been unavoidable. But in this particular case, given that they would have held up the counterattack, such negligence was unforgivable.

They were three hundred metres away. During the sudden lulls in the roaring of the artillery, I could already hear hushed orders being given out. Our men did not utter a squeak, and I myself could feel my fingers itching to squeeze the trigger. Two hundred metres. I shouted the agreed signal, 'Hallo!', and fired the first shot. With the precision of a well-ordered volley, twenty-nine rifles barked out.

Ah, if only I had had a single machine gun! But we managed without. Our men blazed away so furiously that I myself imagined there to be at least two entire companies of us. From each bullet we squeezed all it had to give. The other side had blundered. Instead of immediately hurling themselves against us at our first salvo, they stood still and peered around in every direction. Partly in total darkness and partly in the light of the flickering searchlights which gave human form to trees, bushes, mounds, and stakes, they could not discover in the first minutes whether they were being attacked from the front, from the rear, or from either of their flanks. After that short space of time in which they stood paralyzed, they began to run about in confusion. Immediately there followed the sound of orders, shouts, roars, curses, and whimpers, in no way different to what had befallen our own men scarcely an hour before. We kept up such a steady fire that I could clearly see the yawning gaps beginning to open against the dull sky. Some few came to their senses and threw themselves to the ground and began to return our fire. But this redoubled rate of fire only confused the others even more and made them believe that we were right amongst them.

By now they were deaf to all orders. The rank immediately in front of us began to face about. At first it happened slowly and indecisively; but all of a sudden a stray shell, which might have been one of theirs just as easily as one of ours, burst amongst them and at that point their indecision turned to irreversible flight. The officers screamed out orders in a sharp falsetto and, wherever they themselves were not carried along by the maelstrom, fired their revolvers at the fleeing men, to lend yet further emphasis to their meaningless and insubstantial commands. Increasingly the searchlights were homing in on their positions, because both fronts were searching for the source of the rifle fire. Against the greying dawn sky I could watch the final convulsions of the moribund attack. An officer who was swinging his sword above his head, shouting commands and firing the revolver he held in his other hand, was struck down by a rifle butt wielded by one of his own men. And further to the left another officer was standing alone, abandoned by his troops. He alone was standing motionless against the dawn sky. It was as if he could not grasp what was happening. He was too ashamed to turn and run like his men, and by standing there erect he found a solution which he judged sufficiently honourable.

As it grew lighter, I could observe all the more clearly that the frontal attack they had mounted was on a very extensive scale. But the fleeing centre tore the whole extended line to pieces, destroyed plans, smashed hopes, and made a blundering fool out of a competent general, whose prospect now was that of being guillotined by the tattlers sitting at home. And all because the line had been fired on five hundred metres sooner than they had expected.

Then two of our platoons came marching up. But the only work left for them to do was to gather up the wounded prisoners, of whom there were seventy-eight. We did not count the dead.

My observation post was closed down, because it was not necessary to the spadework of the following two days. The comrades who had helped me were welcomed back to the front line with cheers and congratulations.

To my ears their shouts sounded very far away, for when I got back I stretched myself out on the ground and fell asleep. I dreamt that the sergeant major and the corporal, though they had died long before I found my resting place, were furiously grappling with me and yelling at me, trying to hurl me down into a rocky cleft of giddy depths. But I am unable to say whether they succeeded or not.

By now there were only as many men left in my battalion as would have formed one complete company and two platoons. The missing were either dead, wounded, or prisoners. Not one of my twenty-nine men had been killed, and only five of them had been wounded once again. But none was in danger of losing his life.

It was two days before the heavy cannon and howitzers were brought up. And they did a good job.

One evening, while it was still light, we were ordered on parade. We knew that orders would now be given for the second assault. In the two intervening days the men of our battalion had been overcome by a feverish anxiety that they might no longer be thought worthy of taking part in the second assault. There was also a rumour that that battalion was to be withdrawn entirely and sent home to become the basis of a newly formed replacement battalion. Amongst themselves they were obstinate in their insistence that they would refuse to board the transport. They would not believe that they had been involved in the debacle, and there were not a few of them who maintained in all seriousness that the whole business was untrue and unreal, a figment of the imagination.

But the commanding officer probably thought more highly of them than they had ever credited.

The lieutenant colonel had been killed, and a supernumary major from our battalion was to lead the attack. But that evening the colonel of the regiment came along in person to attend the briefing. He stood in front of the troops and immediately after the major had finished his announcements, he said, 'Good evening, lads!' We did not know what was coming and answered in rather subdued voices, 'Good evening, sir!'

Then he said, 'Men, what happened a few nights ago is not the sort of thing one would expect from German soldiers. But we are only human, and as such we are also subject to human weaknesses. That goes for me, too, when I consider the completely and utterly unsoldierly goings-on that night from the purely human standpoint. But I would immediately add: regarded from the military standpoint, I do not understand it. What is going on here is not some trifling event as far as our nation is concerned; our fatherland is playing for the highest of stakes, namely survival or annihilation. Do not forget it! Who is to protect our country if you do not, if you cannot? The high command had issued an order that you were to be regarded as unreliable and ought not to be brought into a second assault. But because I know you better, I staked my reputation that you would either return as victors or not at all the second time around. Only a fraction of our fine regiment is left, but I am proud to be able to tell you that I have been ordered to lead this unit against the redoubt once more. This allows both you and me the opportunity to win back the honour of our regiment ...'

At this, despite the command of 'Silence in the ranks!', we all gave voice to a rousing cheer.

The colonel went on, '... and to regain the honour of our brave comrades who have fallen, so that they may rest soundly and in peace in their heroes' graves. Do not think that things will be any easier this time around, just because you have heard the roar of our heavy artillery in the meanwhile. Things will be not the least bit easier and you may be sure that only a few of us will come back. And I shall not only be marching before you at your head, I shall also die amongst you. God is on our side! Long live the Regiment! Hurrah!'

Our nervous excitement kept us awake. We marched out at one o'clock at night. By sunrise the next morning, four forts were in our hands, no less than fourteen by midday, and the fortress itself surrendered on the following day.

The victory had cost our regiment dear. When an inspection

was called, there were a great many gaps to be closed before we stood shoulder to shoulder. The colonel was dead, and all but a few of the officers out of action.

But I was alive, with not a scratch on me. Indeed, it was enough to make one lose all faith!

I was assigned to a newly formed battalion, was promoted and awarded the Iron Cross. It was too much for me to bear. I asked to be put on battalion report.

'What is it you want?' asked the major.

'I would like to return my Iron Cross.'

'For what reason?'

'I do not deserve it.'

'What makes you think that?'

'I want to remain an honest man, and as such I have to state that I acted as bravely as I did only because I wanted to commit suicide and therefore placed myself in every exposed position which I thought might offer me the surest opportunity of achieving my purpose.'

'Why don't you want to go on living?'

'Because—well, I can't explain it, sir. You would think my reasons frivolous and unsound. But for me my reasons are absolutely and irrevocably binding.'

'Your reasons really don't have anything to do with the matter, in actual fact. They are entirely your private concern. So I shall not set myself up as your judge or try to hinder you in your plans. Let it be on your own conscience. But you will keep your Cross, and your promotion. What matters to me is that you conducted yourself so bravely that you were the first man I recommended for an award. Your motives are no concern of mine, all that matters to me is your actions. As for the rest, I can tell you that you're out of your mind, young man! Just don't bother me with your foolish nonsense, I shan't have any time for it in future. About turn! Dismiss! Quick march!'

So they would not believe me. They thought me brave, whereas I was far from being so and merely indifferent to everything. Fine, then. I would not allow that to interfere with my purpose, and from that moment on I would raise it to be the governing principle of my life.

My battalion was held in reserve, and I with it. In the meantime they had already taken another redoubt at the front. What a fine opportunity I had missed there! We were moved forward, but were still so far behind the front line that we would scarcely have known there was a war on if we had not seen the shelled and burnt-out towns and villages, and hour by hour had not passed the uncounted masses of fleeing, unresisting inhabitants.

Weeks and weeks went past. Up at the front all kinds of things were happening. A stalemate was reached and nothing moved.

Then there were suddenly whispers and rumours. Nothing definite was known. The news whirled around our heads, crept in between our feet, and hung chokingly in the air. At last there was the pleasant feeling that something somewhere was not as it should have been. But then came second thoughts: what difference does it make to you? After all, the simple fact of knowing about it does nothing to change it. Until finally an inner voice said, Throw all your troubles onto 'them'! The 'them' who're responsible for issuing the orders.

Then, to the shriek of the guns, a start was made on excavating and preparing trenches. At the beginning we had not had much practice at it. No one had thought of such things in peacetime. But when we moved on, we left the trenches behind us. They were to serve as cover in case things did not go according to plan.

We made camp, pitched the tents, cooked our rations, and lay singing around the fire.

Suddenly a man came running from the forward outpost. His face was pale, the fear of death in every line. 'There's water coming! Water coming! A tidal wave! Our outpost has been washed away! The water will be here in three minutes!'

The man was crazed. He shouted and raved. Our captain went over to him and said, 'Look, try to be coherent and tell us what has happened.' The man trembled and shook, then once again shouted with quite unnatural force, 'The water's coming! The water's behind me!'

The captain gave him a swig of brandy from his flask. All of us went to stand around him. The captain said to the lieutenant standing beside him, 'Should we report it to the staff?' 'There's something not right,' said the lieutenant, 'no doubt something has happened. But we're not going to get anything out of that man other than "Water". What I suggest is that we send three men to the guard post at the double.' To this the captain said, 'I'd better send a report of this to the battalion in any case. There might well be some truth in that gibberish.'

Three men leapt to their feet. But while they were fetching their rifles from the stack, we heard shouting off to one side. At first we were confused and thought that the words of the guard, now lying on the ground with his eyes closed, were ringing in our ears. But then we heard more and more clearly, 'The water is rising! Flood! Water!'

'Well, damn and blast it again,' said the captain. 'What kind of witches' brew is this? What's going on?'

Then the sergeant major came running past and shouted breathlessly without stopping, 'We're surrounded by floodwaters, sir!'

The captain's jaw dropped slightly, and he smiled half incredulously. But suddenly his smile froze into a grimace. His eyes opened wide, he was incapable of uttering a sound, he staggered slightly, then at once drew himself up again and without saying a word, stretched out his arm and pointed with his index finger.

We turned around and by the light of the setting sun we saw an ocean. An ocean, where only an hour before there had been dry land. It was such an awesome sight that we all stood there as if paralyzed. The setting sun cast its blood-red reflection onto the ocean, and we could see that it was boundless, for there was nothing but water as far as the distant horizon behind which the sun was disappearing, its lower edge dipping into the ocean.

For one moment there was a deathly hush in the camp, and through the silence we heard the gurgle of the lapping water. It came closer, only to give ground again. First it would make a tentative advance, and only then seize final possession. But though the first wave might slip back in tentative uncertainty, the next held its ground and did not yield what it had won, while the next wave again was already hard on its heels. It came on with such an irresistible, irreversible omnipotence that we all shared the same initial feeling: useless to run from it, it may not get us at once, but it will get us all the same, even if we were to run to the ends of the earth! Behind us there remained a narrow strip of dry ground which would allow us to make good our escape in the meantime.

In calm, unruffled, and habitual tones the order had already been sounded: 'Strike camp, prepare to march!' Immediately after: 'Shoulder your weapons!' The officers and NCOs hurried through the bustle and scurry of the camp to make sure that nothing was left behind.

By now we were standing with our feet in pools and puddles. The captain was studying the map and shaking his head all the while. It seemed that he was momentarily at a loss to know which direction to turn to; for there was not only the water to be reckoned with, off to one side the enemy stood waiting for us, of that we could be sure.

The adjutant came dashing up from battalion headquarters. Our report had just arrived and had not been understood. But being on horseback, the adjutant had seen that we had struck camp and were already up to our ankles in the ocean. 'Try to join up with the battalion!' he shouted from the saddle, and raced back at the gallop. But when we arrived at the battalion's position, there was no longer anything to be seen of it; only trampled cooking-trenches, charred wood, and empty ration tins.

To add to our difficulties it was pitch-dark by now. We followed the clearly beaten track left by the battalion and late in the night happened on a communications patrol, which had itself lost touch with base. Our beautifully dug trenches offered no obstruction to the progress of our retreat, for they had not been prepared with such an enemy in mind. Still, we made more haste than the water. And that was our good fortune.

For weeks on end we have been stationed in one and the same position. Forty-eight hours in the trenches, forty-eight hours in barns, barracks, outhouses, cellars, and half-derelict buildings. We have made intimate friends of the rats. We came to an unwritten agreement with them: as long as they did not insist upon too physical a proximity, we would leave them alone. In the event, we lost out by this agreement, however subtly we framed its various articles, for we were in an alarming minority. Eventually they became so attached to us that they followed us right up to the front line, and because of the excellent attention we bestowed on them there, they founded new nations.

The other side was apparently expecting that we would undertake some sort of action. But we had no thought of doing so. For quite some time we had it easy where we were. As far as I was concerned, we could stay there quite happily until judgement day. If the other side had no interest in throwing us out of their country, then we certainly had none in leaving of our own accord. So there was some bored skirmishing now and again. We stood by our rifles, hands in our pockets, peered out at the countryside through a narrow hole, and smoked one cigar after another. They did just the same on the other side. With bow and arrow we shot complimentary messages across to one another. Those from the other side unfailingly began with the letter 'M', ours with 'L'. But in the long run that ceased to amuse us. We became more cultivated and bombarded each other with newspapers. On both sides we hunted out those which could be calculated to give the greatest pleasure to our opposite numbers. In doing so we avoided a great deal of embarrassment, since the bitterest word is always the true one. When someone was occasionally incautious enough to let himself be seen, it was regarded as an offence against good manners to start blasting away at once.

However; they sent us a raw lieutenant, a reservist. It had taken him all that time to find his way into the country through Switzerland, and he had not the remotest notion of what war was really like. He had not become acclimatized yet and put a very precise value on his own life. Much more so than we. We went for walks along the embankment, sat for a few minutes on the rim of the trench to give our bones a brief well-deserved rest, strolled with raised heads to our rabbit hutch and collected grass and weeds behind our trench to give to the animals; we climbed onto the parapet, squinted contentedly at the sun as if we were in our own backyards, and waited impatiently for the kitchen orderlies, who would be having a nap somewhere along the way so that we would not scald our tongues on the hot pease-pudding. By and large, we acted as though we pitied no one in the wide world more than the snipers on the other side. And over there they did exactly the same. Depending on the state of things, sometimes it would be our gunners who began to fret, and sometimes theirs.

But the new reservist lieutenant, 'the foreigner', still had no poetic vein for such sports. He thought them stupid and needless and one day said something about 'depriving the fatherland of its valuable human resources in an unnecessary manner.' And he was entirely right. But as I mentioned, he was still not acclimatized; he lacked the poetic flair which was the only thing that made life at all bearable, if one was not to succumb to dullness of mind.

A very young colour-bearer with the shining eyes and rosy cheeks of adolescence was crouching on the parapet with his legs dangling over the edge, rolling a smoking cigarette back and forth between his teeth and in general inviting the other side to take abundant measure of his backside. 'Well, sir,' he said, 'if you want to feel the golden glow of the morning sun, there's no other way to go about it. You can scarcely expect the jolly old chap up there to scramble down into our stinking sewer. You have to make the effort to climb out of it. But there you are, some people know when to stop and others don't. That's their nature and there's just nothing people can do about their natures.'

The lieutenant pressed his lips together to show that he understood well enough. Then he craned his head over the parapet, so that the tip of his cap might just have been visible from the other side. A second later the lieutenant pitched backwards. He had been shot through the head.

'But, sir—' the colour-bearer called quite uncomprehendingly, as he leapt down from the parapet and put his arm around the lieutenant's shoulders, saying over and over again, 'But, sir, I didn't mean it like that. Why won't you listen, sir, I didn't mean it like that at all.'

Even so, the lieutenant was already dead.

It's beyond my understanding, too. I can hold my head above the parapet the whole day through, exercise my legs on the embankment and who knows what else, they always shoot past me. Purely out of spite.

Well, things took a turn for the better. Just as I wanted them to. We could not be relieved, and only once in two days had we anything to eat. Our retreat was cut off by bursting shells. Six kitchen orderlies had been killed. By then there was nothing else for it but to hold out. Not even the Kaiser could have been come to our aid. That night we got some bread and a messtin half-full of slop with bits of meat in it. More kitchen orderlies were killed. The telephone line was put out of action.

'Who will volunteer to repair the line?' the lieutenant asked. I stepped forward together with another soldier. I knew precisely why I was volunteering. But the soldier, so he told me, was doing it because it had to be done and because a very great deal could depend upon the state of the line. In his case it really was patriotism, and I felt annoyed that the same could not be said of me. But everyone believed that it was extraordinarily brave of me to undertake the task, since it could have been done just as well by a couple of privates. She was the reason, none other than she; yet on reflection it was not she after all. Rather, it was something which lay outside our mastery, because we had no conception of it.

Naturally, the damaged section of the line lay in the middle of the firing zone, otherwise it could not have been damaged, seeing that the line was buried underground. The soldier did not even make it as far as the break in the line. His leg was taken off. He felt no pain and lay there quite quietly with his eyes wide open. I told him that I would drag him back to the trench on my return. His joy was unbounded. Anything rather than lie alone and wounded in the field! I found the break, connected the wires and made sure they were well insulated, then buried the line again. There were so many shell splinters round about that it looked like a stony field. After that I managed to get the soldier back to the trench. We bound his wound tightly. With any luck he would be able to hold out for twenty-four hours.

On the other side they were preparing to attack. In the complete certainty of success. When it came to the point, why should not they, too, have some cause to celebrate for once. We had so often done so, and always at their expense. In a few places our trench had collapsed. But in the main it was proof against shells, and so far we had suffered no losses. They began slyly, one had to grant them that. Nor did their barrage allow even a single squad of reinforcements to be brought up to the line. They thought that we had already been softened to a pulp, but they would find themselves with bloody noses. We had stopped firing hours before. Down the telephone came orders and instructions which made it clear to us that no one had any confidence in our ability to hold the position. Sometimes even the very greatest bravery is not enough.

The shelling of our trenches petered out gradually, then suddenly leapt far to the rear of our line, as if regulated by the clock. So we knew what to expect next. Over there they were leaping over the parapets and scrambling through the narrow openings in the wire, before spreading out into an extended line to advance in dispersed groups. The sunlight flickered on their polished bayonets. Two, three, four ranks in succession.

By now we could make out their faces quite clearly and see whether they were young or old fellows. Most of them were fairly old.

A hundred and fifty metres. Our machine guns began to clatter. Sleepily for the first few shots, as they had done during basic training. But after that! We stood in the trench and aimed with a calmness which we ourselves thought astonishing. The calmness of extreme danger. We knew that each miss lessened our chances of survival by one degree. The other side were at a disadvantage: they could not shoot, only run. And they were running into our gunsights. The first rank, the second, the third. They broke formation, faltered, raced forward. But they did not turn and run. Not one of them. They were tough and brave and kept on coming. This tenacity, these unstoppable hordes, drained the confidence of our men. It was noticeable in their nervous and too hurried shooting. Only the machine guns kept up their montonous rhythm. Which is what machines are for.

Now they were twenty paces from our wire. A few of them were out in front, cutting the strands and trampling them underfoot. Then at last the captain's whistle shrilled through the air. The colour-bearer was first onto the parapet. I have my suspicions that he had already positioned himself halfway up, otherwise he could not have managed it. In an instant we scrambled out. All of us. And we were not few in number. Things happened so fast that many of us became entangled in our own wire, because they failed to see the lanes in their haste. Now the advantage was ours once more. The other side was out of breath, and completely surprised at that, by our breakout and our large numbers. We pressed them steadily back. It was a slow business, but before long they were fighting in their own trenches. They retreated further, to their second line of trenches. Here they made a stand, and we had to turn back, withdrawing even beyond their forward trench. It would have been impossible to hold, since it was heavily outflanked on both sides.

Then we were in our own trench once again, totally exhausted, yet convinced that they would not attempt a second attack either on that day or on the next. It was too costly a game.

The colour-bearer was caught on the wire in front of their first line. We thought that he was dead, but suddenly someone who had been looking through his glasses for a while said, 'He's still alive!' Then we stood watching the poor fellow thrash about. He was wounded and unable to disentangle himself. Over there they did not care at all. The captain also watched for a while, until he said, with gravity etched into his face, 'There's only one thing for it; so which of you has a spark of pity for the boy and is willing to make it quick for him?' He averted his eyes from us while saying this and stared at the ground in front of his feet. The colour-bearer waved and pointed to his heart. We understood only too well what both the captain and the colour-bearer were trying to say, and knew even then how grateful we ourselves would have been for that small spark of pity in such a situation. We waited for the shot. But it was not fired, and instead of it everyone seemed to be expecting a miracle. And over there the man writhed, so that the blood rushed to our heads and none of us had the courage to look any longer.

At all events it made no difference to me. I had no intention of celebrating my return home, or of making a fresh start on some kind of nonsensical daily round after the war. And why should I have been the one to prevent the colour-bearer from committing a mountain of follies later on? He was still without any knowledge of life; and the greatest thing that exists had so far occupied only the fantasies of his sleeping or waking hours, which he would wean himself from once he came to know the real thing. He was just the kind of person who would want to go on living and embroil himself in a great deal of foolishness. For foolishness alone is the spice of life. I did not see why I should not change places with him in some acceptable way. Philosophers are the most superfluous

of men. Even more so once the war is over, for then there will be
time only for working and dancing.

'I'll bring him in,' I said aloud, to save anyone else from pity.
They all stared at me, obviously thinking that my mental faculties
had been impaired during the attack, for it was sheer madness, and
doomed to fail into the bargain.

An actor on stage can scarcely draw more attention to himself
than a man making his way towards a barbed-wire entanglement
in broad daylight. The second line of trenches, where the other
side had now taken up position, lay only fifty paces beyond the
first. They could get a fine view of me through their sights and use
me for target practice. Indeed, they were blazing away even before
I got close to the wire. It was more than they could have been expecting, and obviously they were competing to see who would score
the hit. Well, that did not need to be any business of mine. And in
any case they were much too excited to loose a well-aimed shot.

The colour-bearer was thoroughly trapped. In his attempts to
crawl out he had got himself completely entangled. Partly I cut
his clothes away, partly I had to snip through the wire as carefully
as I could, since it was caught in his flesh. The boy seemed lifeless
and was covered in blood. He had deep cuts on his hips and thighs.
But they did not appear to be very serious. From the other side
they were contentedly blazing away, though whether from stupidity
or brutality or fear I could not say. The colour-bearer got another
insignificant wound in the calf of his leg. But I got him back to
the trench. He and the man whose leg had been shattered reached
the field hospital in safety that same evening.

Our position was relieved. A fortnight later I was promoted yet
again and given a still higher award for an affair to do with deto-
nating a mine which had seemed nothing out of the ordinary to
me.

I should have left things as they were. But I would have felt
ashamed to accept yet another undeserved award for the bravery
which had been falsely attributed to me. For I had not performed
any act that was worthy of reward, but as always, recently, had
acted from pure self-interest without giving even the most fleeting
thought to duty or love of my country. At all events, my mind was

firmly set on remaining honest, although this idea, too, was beginning to present me with formidable problems.

'You do realize,' the colonel said, 'that strictly speaking you are a deserter and by rights deserve to be brought before a court-martial and sentenced to be shot?'

'No, sir, I was unaware of that, and begging the colonel's pardon, I must protest that I have never at any time considered myself to be a deserter.'

'Anyone who attempts to withdraw himself from his unit while on active service is a deserter. Whatever his manner of running away, whatever his manner of attempting to evade his duty, he is a deserter. The way in which he evades his duty is inconsequential; the intention itself is sufficient to constitute the crime.'

'Excuse me, sir, but if I'm killed, if I had been killed on my very first day in the trenches—'

'Then a higher power would have prevented you from doing the duty which you swore to do in your oath of enlistment, a higher power to which we must all bend the knee and beyond which no one will demand that you should do your duty.'

'In that case a suicide is also a deserter in relation to life.'

'That may be so, but there is no occasion for me to give you my personal opinion on the matter, and only in the most indirect way is it connected with the purely military question which has arisen here.'

'With the greatest respect, sir, I would nevertheless request permission to decline the two decorations and the promotion, since I cannot accept them and remain an honest man.'

'Oh, this is quite ridiculous! Be so good as to spare me such drivel. Your mind doesn't seem to be up to scratch any longer. In that case report to the medical officer, but don't come to me with your scandalous poppycock. Is that understood?'

'Yes, sir!'

'What was your job in civilian life?'

'Philosopher, sir.'

'Oh, I see. Well, that explains a lot. All right, then, you can go. Good day!'

He dismissed me by reaching out his hand and shaking mine.

Maybe we could understand each other better and more easily as human beings than as soldiers.

But with the best will in the world I cannot turn myself inside out. Not for the love of any person or any cause whatsoever, be it ever so noble. There is no compulsion forcing me to adopt as my own the ideals of other people. For example, I might worship where another would spit. Yet that makes me no less a person than any other. Nor am I at all capable of simply falling in behind another, which is why my mental and intellectual world presents a sharp contrast to that of many, perhaps most, other people.

We were transferred to new positions. The troops facing us here were all English.

Soon there was only one weapon we recognized—hand grenades. From time to time, but purely for the sake of a change— gas attacks. Between us was a gigantic mine-crater which had been extended on both sides and made into a quite respectable trench. Sometimes the crater would be in our hands, and we would extend the trench even further; the next time it would be the others who enjoyed possession of the crater, and they, too, would extend the trench. Sometimes the crater would change hands twelve times a day.

Because of an interest, and in order not to lag behind the ordinary soldiers under me, I have been learning to throw grenades. They are the most delightful toys. If they are thrown a tenth of a second too late, then the thrower may find that he is no longer alive and in one piece, whereas to throw them a tenth of a second to early means that someone over there might just stick them in his trouser pockets and nonchalantly stroll around with them until he has a chance to deliver them back to our address.

Someone from the other side came right up to edge of the crater on his own. As it happened, there was no one in the crater. Both of us lay waiting for that auspicious moment when one of us would be the first to move down into the crater and catch the other napping. I was festooned with grenades, and so was he. But I did not stick it out and had to come back. He was better at it than I was, and I soon found out what was meant by good sport. He was alive to all my tricks and snatched up almost every grenade I threw to throw it back to me at once. And of course they exploded on my side, but I gave them a wide berth each time, only because I wanted to be around to see how it would end. We could have amused ourselves like that for hours, with pure and untroubled happiness, but they took the crater and so the show came to an end.

That might have been a fitting occasion to achieve my purpose, but these tedious ups and downs, which had already lasted two weeks, signalling neither victory nor defeat, had driven me to despair.

Under cover of darkness I brought up a machine-gun section with half a platoon of infantry in support. In the morning I discovered that we were cut off. Even with the best will in the world there was no hope of joining up with the battalion, and plainly understandable jeers were already being showered on us from in front and from both sides.

But they would get no joy from me, however long they held their breath, for I least of all had cause to placate them.

There was a reservist amongst us, Heinrich Zietz. He had been away from home since he was called up. He applied for leave and was given ten days so that he could spend some time at home. He belonged to my platoon. Rarely have I seen anyone so overjoyed.

One night we found ourselves in a very isolated outpost, and it was then that he told me all kinds of things about himself and his life at home. He was a metal lathe turner in an engineering works and, from what I could gather, a highly skilled and exceptionally well-paid worker. He was very happy with his wife. She must have been a treasure, and he loved her with a depth of feeling which I had never previously suspected in those of a simple station in life. I had always imagined such finely tuned sensibilities to be the exclusive prerogative of members of the more educated strata of society.

He went off on leave and returned only three days later. He reported to the captain, who was astonished to see him back so soon, for it was much more likely to happen that a man overstayed his leave than that he returned prematurely, something which to the best of my knowledge was completely unprecedented. 'It was just that I wanted to get back to the front and the lads,' he told the captain. 'It's impossible to feel really settled at home, when everything here is touch-and-go.' 'What about your wife? She must have been really delighted to see you home again for a

couple of hours?' 'Yes, of course, sir, that goes without saying.'
And he resumed his place in the ranks.

The day passed in relative tranquillity. The English were waiting, so we waited too. Since they were making no move to attack, we saw no reason to fire off our precious ammunition to no purpose. Who could say how vital every last cartridge might be to us, and for how long? The other side thought they had us in the bag. Taken by and large, we ourselves were not entirely proof against that thought, for I could see not even the remotest possibility of getting ourselves out of the hole we were in for the time being. If they had the time, all they needed to do was to lie back and starve us out. And we did have bread, because we had been expecting a lengthy march and had drawn double iron rations. Best of all, we could fetch drinking water from a stream which flowed through the terrain hard by our position. The machine guns had more need of it than we did.

Nothing in particular happened as the day unfolded. On all sides we heard artillery fire. I put out feelers in every direction, but the result was always the same: all around, not even a mouse could slip through! What was good was that no one in the trenches facing us seemed to have noticed that we were cut off, because on one side the terrain was such that the enemy could not establish whether or not we had a line of communication. In addition, there was no chance that he would be able to overlook our position and so make even a rough estimate of our numbers. In this respect we had a decided advantage.

I slept through the afternoon in order to be wide awake in the evening. At about ten o'clock I set out with three men to see for myself if there was any chance of breaking through. There was only one sector that looked promising, at the point where the enemy lines of communication seemed precarious, the very place where the enemy must have supposed our own line of communication to be.

I assigned the three men to their positions, one far out to the left, the other off to the right, and with the third I kept to the centre. This last was Heinrich Zietz. About half an hour later we made contact with the other side. They were firing candle bombs at long intervals, but in rather a lackadaisical way. It gave the impression that they were doing it purely for practice. For twice in succession we were both silhouetted against the flare of light, yet not a trigger twitched. In any case the observer would have been daydreaming about some football match or other which his team had won. And the others could not have cared less.

By then we were very close to the sentry post. When the wind chanced to blow in our direction, our nostrils filled with Navy Cut, until the light evening breeze veered by a few points and we smelt Player's Honeydew Gold Leaf. It woke incomparable memories of peacetime, of hunts and fireside gatherings in the Scottish Highlands, of evenings spent half in reverie and half in pleasant conversation by the Nile.

I examined my compass. But the luminous dots confused me, so I switched on my torch. Zietz screened it with his cap. He was lying close beside me, the map spread out in front of us. I took out my pencil to make some notes and to this end gave the torch to Zietz. As I was handing it to him, a warm drop of moisture rolled onto the back of my hand. I looked up and noticed that the tears were steaming from his eyes. I said nothing, and he did not notice that I had observed him.

Then we moved further forward under cover of darkness. The candlebombs stopped coming, but the first of the enemy sentries were so close ahead of us that we had to begin making our way back again. I had seen what I wanted to see and knew that it could be done.

But we did not go far; now that we were here anyway and behind us there was nothing that we could usefully do for the moment, we remained where we were. And it was at least possible that we might still learn something which would be of help to us in one way or another.

For a long time we lay side by side. I was thinking of his bitter tears, and after a long silence I said to Zietz, 'So what did she say?' He could not speak. However, I heard him muffle a shudderingly painful sob, though I pretended not to have noticed. I did not want to humiliate him.

It was a fine spring night, a night full of dreams, of longings, of hope for life. From far to the rear the thunder of gunfire rolled towards us. It seemed to come from another world and made one feel so happy to be far away from the war; let them wage war to their heart's content there in the rear, on that other continent. So distant and far away and forlorn did the thunder sound. Someone on the other side was playing the banjo, and occasionally the monotonous cadence of a Canadian song came to our ears. The earth was breathing as deeply and narcotically as a woman in the expectation of fulfilment.

Then something burst within him and he could no longer hold back.

'You can't imagine how much I was looking forward to my leave. Nowhere in the world could you have found a happier and more blissfully married couple. We loved each other as though we had been married only a fortnight before. Her letters overflowed with tenderness and longing. I did not send her word that I was coming home on leave. For I did not want to share the joy of our meeting with anyone but myself. It was nine in the evening when I arrived. I raced up the stairs, since I had seen a light in the window from outside and knew she was at home, a good omen, I thought, for she might just as easily have been out somewhere. I had to stand outside her door and get my breath back, my heart was in my throat. I rang the bell, and heard her coming to the door. She opened it. There was a bright light in the hallway. She saw me standing there and didn't know what to say. I began to feel ill at ease, as if I were standing in front of a stranger, and I smiled. But I had the impression that this smile was distorting my face into a grotesque caricature. I said, 'Well, isn't this a surprise?'' She just went on staring at me and obviously couldn't make up her mind whether to let me in or not. But though she still didn't say anything, she opened the door wider and let me in. Then she walked ahead of me towards the kitchen, and I followed. She was standing by the table, irresolutely, looking at me. Then I went over to her and embraced her. She let it happen, but did not respond to my kiss. Suddenly I felt myself a stranger in my own home, the home we shared. Why, I could not tell. Then she said, "Do you want to stay here tonight?" It was some time before the enormity of her question sank into my mind. At first I imagined she was thinking that perhaps I had only dropped in for an hour or so while passing through on my way to another front. I said, "I've been given ten days' leave, that's really something, isn't it? I'm the first one in our company who's been given leave." "Well," she answered, "then I suppose I'd better make a clean breast of it: I've met another man and we've fallen very much in love with one another. He's been coming to see me for the past five weeks and he's—he's next door in the sitting room." I wanted to sit down but felt that I would dirty myself if I happened to sit on the chair he might have used. To find out just where I stood and what rights I still had in my own house, which I'd bought and paid for in full out of my own wages, I asked, "So I suppose he'll be staying here this evening, and perhaps even longer than that?" And to that her reply was, "But I've just told you that we've fallen very much in love with one another; surely you can work the rest out for yourself. It's not as if you're a child any longer. It's not as if you were born yesterday."

'I looked at my former wife once more and then left without saying another word. When I was on the stairs, she came running after me and called out in a low voice, "Heinrich, don't leave me like that, at least tell me that you're not angry with me." But without turning my head I went on down the stairs.

'Down in the entrance hall I stood leaning against the wall and wept like a little boy. In that one moment I had lost everything I possessed: my home, parents, desires, faith in people, every last thing, for to me she had been everything that made life worth living. Then I walked to the station and lay on a bench in the waiting room until the next train left for the front. And here I am. I know that I'll find my lost home again. All the rest means nothing to me any longer. So now you can probably imagine what state of mind I am in.'

It would be hard to find anyone who could imagine it better than myself. And now I had discovered the man I would need at some point within the next few days. For he stuck to his guns and was absolutely reliable right to the bitter end. Indeed, he had nothing to lose, but everything to win.

On the following two nights we went out again and I grew more and more confident that my plan would work. If it was at all feasible, then it would have to be here on this narrow strip of land.

On the last night I was accompanied by several men who fitted

fuses to the large number of land mines we had improvised from
our supplies and buried them over a wide area, at a place where
we would need to hold off an attack from the flank for the brief
space of a quarter of an hour, to enable us to turn the other flank
and clear a path for the breakout.

I gave command of the left flank to the sergeant major. To
cover all eventualities I briefed him on my plans. But if I did not
succeed at my own position, the whole plan would fall through;
in the first place the other side would realize then that here was
an unsecured breach lying open to them, and in the second we
could not hold out for a further two days without hunger driving
us to surrender.

Zietz and I were the first to go. Five minutes after they had
been changed, the eight sentries who could have been most
dangerous to us had been wiped out. Before the next relief arrived
or a round might be expected, we would be well under way.
Quietly we brought the machine guns into position. Several men
stood by every gun, ready to drag it away at the given moment,
since it would have been so much wasted effort to take the car-
riages with us. The sergeant major was on the left with two machine
guns. The hardest going would be on our right. Here Zietz and
myself manned the gun. It was in our favour that a fairly heavy
bombardment began to our rear. It seemed that a rescue attempt
was being undertaken on our account, always supposing they
did not believe that we had been put in the bag long before. Our
machine gun started to fire, making it so hot for the other side
that they retreated without putting up a fight, to put some distance between us and get a clearer view of the situation.

'Zietz,' I said, 'someone must attend to the mines now. If they
won't detonate, try a match, but they must explode, otherwise
we're finished; take a look over there, we've managed to smoke
them out where we are, but they've already got wind of the
whole scheme and if they come at us from the rear, we'll never
shake them off our tails. When the mines have gone off, follow
up at once with hand grenades. One man can do it. In the darkness they won't be able to see whether they're up against a whole
platoon or just one man. I don't suppose you'll make it back
again, Zietz. Do you want to go through with it?'

'I'll do it, and you can be sure I'll do it well.'

'All right, off you go. And Zietz, if we shouldn't see one another again, God be with you.' 'Thanks, and the same to you.'

I stayed behind as much as I could, since those in front were already at the river and as good as in safety, and I wanted a last chance to take Zietz with me, if it could still be managed and he was still alive. As I heard the mines booming behind me, the last machine gun was dragged past, followed by two sections of soldiers who were firing as they went. I was the last. I could still hear Zietz's hand grenades. But then, far to the rear, amongst the enemy who had now broken through on the flank in the place where Zietz must have been, I saw by the light of a rocket the body of a man thrown into the air in a peculiarly sprawling leap. That meant a bullet through the head. He had found his way home.

For a good thirty minutes we had to force a way for ourselves and the machine guns through water which came up to our chests. Then our route led us up a miserably steep and difficult wooded incline which seemed just as endless. Once at the top, we could at last rest for a while. The sun was already above the horizon. And only then did I discover to my astonishment that those of our men who had been in the lead had dragged with them four-teen prisoners onto whom they had loaded the machine guns. They themselves had been walking alongside, quite at their leisure.

And I was still alive and was promoted again.

This time I said nothing. What purpose would it have served? No one underderstood, and if anyone were to understand, then he would not admit it.

But a German ought to understand.

Today I was presented to the commander-in-chief. He studied me attentively for some time, but said nothing, simply offered me his hand, shook hands twice, firmly, then nodded his head pensively, looking at me all the while, as if he wanted to ask me something but could not think what it might be. I felt mortally ashamed when I recognized something akin to cool admiration in his glance. I would have liked to shout aloud that I did not want to lie, above all not to this man, and that I was far from being the bravest of all possible fellows as everyone imagines me to be, as everyone says when they see me. But what can I do to stop it!

Yet one single person is bound to know the truth, the only one who will believe it, because she understands. I do not want to carry my lie with me on my unexplored pathway. Perhaps this person, the only one who means enough to me that I can share with her my thoughts and my feelings, will one day succeed in proving that in not one fibre of my being was I a hero, and that there might well be other motives for heroism in battle than those which are commonly ascribed. One fine day far into the future, when present notions about human heroism will have been completely overturned.

To her I shall send this book. When she holds it in her hands, she will know that I am gone; that I could not stay, because she was my life and I lost this life. The man who still breathed after that portentous hour was merely a machine. For all my actions since that hour have been the actions of complete insensibility. For only he who loves life above all else, who is now and always will be totally and unremittingly sensible of the dangers which surround him, to their fullest extent and in their most horrendous potentialities, only he who concedes to every other person from the plainest conviction, the same rights as to himself, yet nonetheless encounters all of these dangers with eyes wide open, only he may say of himself that he is truly a hero. Who calls the child brave that plays with wolves!

On the day when I first recognize that my actions are of significance to a cause greater and higher than my own, my life will be fulfilled.

And he whose life is fulfilled, dies.

Before then no man dies, not even in battle.

Day after day after day... thought following upon thought... Chasing, hunting, tormenting, stumbling after one another in untiring perplexity. And in between, pitiless as the tolling of a bell, eternal, the loudest and most distressing: Why? For what? Why? For what?

Came an evening at last. I was in the front line, in a foxhole. Quite alone. A man came running towards me, tossed me a sealed order: At fifteen hundred tomorrow!

Now I am alone again. Over on the other side the sun is going to its rest. In a molten blaze of glory. Above me cranes pass by in narrow wedges like the shades of the forgotten.

From somewhere behind me the fading sound of an accordian: My sweetheart and me! A crow, its black wings flapping clumsily over the wasteland, caws and soars and is lost to sight.

And suddenly I know: there is nothing more for me to say. The consummation has been reached. In my life and in myself. All my thoughts go out to her. Tomorrow death will come. It can take nothing from me, since there is nothing more to take and all its questing is in vain.

Now at last it is I who stand triumphant!

Translator's Note

Ret Marut made his debut as a writer in 1912, in the pages of the *Düsseldorfer Zeitung*. A further ten of his stories appeared in provincial newspapers in the following two years. None of these early stories appears in this collection.

Of the stories translated here into English, 'Mother Beleke' was first published in the Leipzig-based magazine *Reclams Universum*, in July 1915. (An abbreviated version appeared the following year in an anthology of war stories from the same publisher.) 'The Unknown Soldier' and 'In the Fog' appeared in 1915 and 1916 respectively in the weekly magazine *März* (Berlin/Munich). *Reclams Universum* accepted 'The Silk Scarf' in 1917, while 'The Story of a Nun' was published in *Westermanns Monatshefte* of Brunswick in 1918.

To the Honourable Miss S... appeared as a separate volume in 1916. The publisher was given as Irene Mermet, who was Marut's companion during his years in Munich. The remaining stories were not published until 1919, when Marut brought out a collection of satirical pieces under the title *The BLue-Speckled SParroW. Burlesques, Sketches, and Tales, Published by the Ziegelbrenner.* Included here, along with the title story, 'The BLue-Speckled SParroW', are 'Originality', 'The Art of the Painter', 'A Writer of Serpentine Shrewdness', 'My Visit to the Writer Pguwlkschrj Rnfajbzxlquy', 'Titles', 'The Kind of Thing That Can Happen in France', 'Deceivers', and 'The Actor and the King'.